FAKING A DATE WITH HER COWBOY BOSS

MILLER BROTHERS OF TEXAS BOOK FIVE

NATALIE DEAN

DEDICATION

I'd like to dedicate this book to YOU! The readers of my books. Without your interest in reading these heartwarming stories of love, I wouldn't have made it this far. So thank you so much for taking the time to read any and hopefully all of my books.

And I can't leave out my wonderful mother, son, sister, and Auntie. I love you all, and thank you for helping me make this happen.

Most of all, I thank God for blessing me on this endeavor.

OTHER BOOKS BY NATALIE DEAN

Miller Family Saga

BROTHERS OF MILLER RANCH

Miller Family Saga Series 1

Her Second Chance Cowboy

Saving Her Cowboy

Her Rival Cowboy

Her Fake-Fiance Cowboy Protector

Taming Her Cowboy Billionaire

Brothers of Miller Ranch Complete Collection

MILLER BROTHERS OF TEXAS

Miller Family Saga Series 2

The New Cowboy at Miller Ranch Prologue

Humbling Her Cowboy

In Debt to the Cowboy

The Cowboy Falls for the Veterinarian

Almost Fired by the Cowboy

Faking a Date with Her Cowboy Boss

Miller Brothers of Texas Complete Collection

BRIDES OF MILLER RANCH, N.M.

Miller Family Saga Series 3

Cowgirl Fallin' for the Single Dad

Cowgirl Fallin' for the Ranch Hand

Cowgirl Fallin' for the Neighbor

Cowgirl Fallin' for the Miller Brother

Cowgirl Fallin' for Her Best Friend's Brother

Cowboy Fallin' in Love Again

Brides of Miller Ranch Complete Collection

Miller Family Wrap-up Story

(An update on all your favorite characters!)

Copper Creek Romances

BAKER BROTHERS OF COPPER CREEK

Copper Creek Romances Series 1

Cowboys & Protective Ways

Cowboys & Crushes

Cowboys & Christmas Kisses

Cowboys & Broken Hearts

Cowboys & Second Chances

Cowboys & Wedding Woes

Cowboys' Mom Finds Love

Baker Brothers of Copper Creek Complete Collection

CALLAHANS OF COPPER CREEK

Copper Creek Romances Series 2

Making a Cowgirl

Marrying a Cowgirl

Christmas with a Cowgirl

Trusting a Cowgirl

Dating a Cowgirl

Catching a Cowgirl

Loving a Cowgirl

Marrying a Cowboy

Callahans of Copper Creek Complete Collection

KEAGANS OF COPPER CREEK

Copper Creek Romances Series 3

Some Cowboys are Off-Limits

Some Cowgirls Love Single Dads

Some Cowboys are Infuriating

Some Cowboys Don't Like City Girls

Some Cowboys Heal Broken Hearts

Some Cowgirls are Worth Protecting

Some Cowboys are Just Friends (Coming August 2024)

Though I try to keep this list updated in each book, you may also visit my website nataliedeanauthor.com for the most up to date information on my book list.

CONTENTS

Chapter 1 . . . 1
Chapter 2 . . . 14
Chapter 3 . . . 33
Chapter 4 . . . 45
Chapter 5 . . . 53
Chapter 6 . . . 65
Chapter 7 . . . 78
Chapter 8 . . . 87
Chapter 9 . . . 93
Chapter 10 . . . 105
Chapter 11 . . . 116
Chapter 12 . . . 128
Chapter 13 . . . 142
Chapter 14 . . . 155
Chapter 15 . . . 165
Chapter 16 . . . 175
Chapter 17 . . . 186
Chapter 18 . . . 201
Chapter 19 . . . 217
Chapter 20 . . . 221

Leilani's Epilogue . . . 231
Simon's Epilogue . . . 237
About the Author . . . 243

1

———————

Simon

Simon sipped at his cool coffee, eyes out the window as he observed the rush hour traffic, both in the streets and on foot. He hadn't been in such a crowded city in a while and was enjoying just watching the people and vehicles go by.

He was familiar with the small diner he was sequestered in, the aged walls and outdated paraphernalia on the walls echoing back to when he was a senior in high school. Back then, he and his friends thought that visiting some of the poorer areas of the city was some sort of daring escapade, something they would talk about for a week or two. Adventures that left them strutting around the high school like they owned the place.

Although technically, McLintoc Miller did have an entire

wing at the school named after him and the Whitaker family had the school's theater bearing their own name.

But tax-write offs aside, the nostalgia of it all was nice. It reminded him of a simpler time, one when the world was so very big but also very black and very white.

Currently, most things seemed to be a dull shade of gray.

Not in the literal sense, he'd been around the world and back, seen magnificent cities, eaten delicious foods. He'd stayed in five-star resorts and had slept on dirt floors. He'd met rich, poor, local celebrities and beggars. He'd learned so much from them, taught a few things here and there, and had experiences that most could only dream of.

...and now he was in a place where most people's lives would never extend beyond their own doorstep.

If he wasn't in public, maybe he would have chuckled at how small that existence was. Actually, probably not. It wasn't like he was in the best mood.

How could he be? He was back home, about to rejoin his family. If there were any people who had small worlds, it was them. So wrapped up in their ranch, tensions running high between all of them. It was small-minded and exhausting, and Simon just wished that they could see beyond it.

There was a whole world out there where mergers didn't matter. Or stocks. Or anything of the sort. But none of them knew anything about that. The Millers, even their cousins up north and to the west, were so wrapped up in their little slices of life that the rest of the world might not even exist.

That was why he'd wanted to get away in the first place. Being the youngest, he'd gotten to see what happened when his older brothers tried to branch out, to explore and find out who they were. Each one of them had been smacked down and assimilated into the company like it was some sort of ravenous animal that couldn't be satisfied. Sure, his brothers were *good* at what they did, but they all became such copies of each other, all vying for Dad's barely there attention, that Simon didn't want that to happen to *him*.

He'd graduated high school early, then took a gap-year to shadow his dad's connections at several different companies all across the state. He watched, he learned, and it was enough to figure out that he didn't want to be another peon to his dad. He wanted to forge his own path.

So, he'd gone to college. Gotten his Associate's degree, then his Bachelor's. And then he'd applied for a Master's program. He'd even changed his major twice, but even with all of that and nearly a year spent wandering the world, he was still twenty-four and moving back home.

He supposed it was his own fault for taking summer classes to get ahead and nearly maxing out on his class credits every semester, but it was one of the few ways to stay away from home but still keep his parents pleased. Mom loved that he'd always been bookish, or gifted, as some of his teachers called him. And it sure did look good for Dad to have a son who excelled academically and could make scholastic connections in another state.

"Hey there, hun," his server said, breaking his line of thought as she approached his table with a sweet smile.

She was somewhere in either her late twenties or early thirties, her hair up in a brown bun with two pencils stuck into it. She'd been friendly enough since he'd sat down—if a bit too talkative—so he pasted a smile across his face. There weren't many rules for him in his life, but being kind to wait staff was always one of them.

She continued, "It's time for my break, so one of the lovelies here is going to finish up your meal so you don't have to rush. You look like you're relaxing real good here."

He glanced at his phone, the time tattling that he'd been there for at least an hour, just drinking things and never ordering his meal yet. In his journey, he'd heard servers complain about "campers," folks who overstayed at tables and cost them tips as well as customer real estate, so he set his coffee down and held up a finger for her to wait.

"One moment," he said, shooting her a friendly smile before fishing a twenty from his wallet.

"Oh, you don't have to do that love, our breaks are—"

"It's fine. I'd like to. I haven't ordered much, and I know I'm taking up a good table. Please, it's yours."

"You sure? We split tips and all of us are friends here so—"

But Simon was already missing his quiet contemplation. "Please, consider it a thank-you for the space."

"Well, I'm not one to look a gift horse in the mouth! Thank you, love, you have a good day." She gave a wink that rode on the correct line between friendly and flirty, then happily walked off.

Once she was gone, Simon settled back and returned to his thoughts.

He fully realized that he was postponing heading back to the estate because he was dreading it. He knew he needed to eventually, if only to figure out what he was going to do next and make sure his bank account stayed filled.

One would think that after nearly a year traveling the world and seeing a lifetime's worth of adventure, something would have inspired him, given him a direction. But even after all of those months of experiencing, learning, questioning, he was just as directionless as before. His trip was over, and he had nothing to do. No purpose.

Perhaps that was one of the reasons he resented his family so sharply. Their worlds were tiny, yes. Silly, vapid, self-centered, but all of them seemed to have found a reason to *be*. Samuel had run off with a farmhand and they were happily living on Aunt Annie's ranch. Solomon was involved in several housing projects for the poor, Silas had his community center, Sterling had his animal and soil projects. Even Sal had found something. Sure, that something came in the form of a long-legged British woman with a real set of cheekbones, but they seemed to be doing well together and Sal had settled down.

Which was good. If there was one thing Simon felt guilty for, it was abandoning the brother he was closest to. Sal had always been a bit of a reedy guy, not very strong or smart or well-spoken, but he'd always been kind. When his older brother had suddenly started putting on muscle and becoming some sort of heartthrob, young Simon hadn't known what to think about any of that situation and they'd drifted apart.

But that probably wouldn't have happened if Sal had been willing to forget about pleasing their dad and the Miller brand, but he hadn't been, so what was done was done.

"Hello there! I'm sure Becky already told you that you were getting a new server today, but here I am."

Simon blinked and looked to the person talking to him. She was wearing the standard uniform of the diner, black pants with a blue blouse and white, dotted apron, her full lips pulled wide in what seemed to be a genuine smile.

"I'm Leilani, by the way," she continued. Her voice was different than what he expected. A bit lower, a bit raspier, but not in an unflattering way. Just... unique enough to catch his notice. "And can I get you some food to go along with your two coffees, two beers and three glasses of water that you've been nursing since you got here?"

"Oh, you've been watching me enough to know all that I've ordered?"

"I'd love to say I have, but Becky transferred your table over to me, so I got to see what you've been up to."

"Did you just reveal an insider secret to me?" he said, flashing her one of his winning grins. He hadn't traveled around the entire world a couple of times without learning to be charming. Plus, charisma seemed to run in the Miller family, even if his family seemed to turn theirs off whenever dealing with someone below their economic class.

Granted, that had mostly eased off with his brothers all becoming involved with either employees or random women they'd met from unusual places. Simon wasn't sure how *that* happened, but he was sure there were interesting stories behind it all.

Maybe one day he would sit down and ask his siblings about it. But for the moment, he was in the diner without a single sibling around.

"No, nothing so important. A true secret would be what brands we mix in the ketchup bottle when we refill them at the end of the night." She flashed her own cheeky grin, and Simon found himself leaning forward.

She looked young, maybe around his age, with tanned skin and her long, long, dark hair carefully braided and hanging down behind her. She was tall, for a woman, somewhere just below six foot if he had to guess and had a generous sort of figure that might have been called fat by some but Simon considered healthy and attractive. Her gray eyes were observing him with a keen sort of light that he was sure drew plenty of people in, and as he looked closer, he realized that there were little flecks of gold and brown within those pools.

Latina, maybe? But something about the features didn't add up. Simon had been around the world and seen plenty of people, but she reminded him more of folks he'd seen in Australia and New Zealand rather than anyone from Mexico, Puerto Rico or any other Latin countries.

"Ketchup, huh? And what kind of price tag does that kind of secret come with?"

"Not for sale," she quipped right back, her cheeks filling as her grin grew. "But you know what is? Any of our specialty pancakes, milkshakes and burgers. You can always add an extra patty for just two dollars, and we now have veggie burgers made in house."

"Do I look like someone who eats veggie burgers?"

"I make it a habit not to try to guess what someone might or might not eat by the look of them." And then that broad grin curled at the end, giving her a sort of impish expression that made him want to lean forward and find out what other mischief she could get up to in just a few words. "Because, if I did, I'd assume that half of our salsas and hot sauces are out of your league."

"Are you saying I can't handle the heat?"

"Of course not. Just giving an example of an assumption one might make when a handsome guy with golden skin, but bone-white tan lines, comes into their diner."

She didn't miss a single beat, her eyes flicking over him and lingering on his wrist, where his watch had stood before he'd taken it off for the airport, then flicking to the undone button on his shirt, where the tiniest bit of pale white stood out under his backpacking tan.

"Bone white, huh?"

"Well, I could say porcelain, but I've found most guys don't like being compared to something dolls are made out of."

"Technically, all of us come from dolls, right?"

"Dolls?" There it was, the tiniest flash of uncertainty before it seemed to click behind her eyes. "Right, mainlander slang. You mean women with that, right? But all cutesy and southern."

Simon attached mock offense to his tone, giving her a dramatic look. "What? Are you saying you're not a local?" He'd known that from the moment she opened her mouth. She *did* have an accent, one that was mild and made her words come more from the back of her throat, but it wasn't like any he'd ever heard from his friends or family. "How am I supposed to trust your opinion on what's good at this here local diner?"

Her hand went to her belly, where it patted several times with a sense of finality. Simon tried not to let his gaze linger too long on the action, but he couldn't help but wonder just how soft that part of her might me.

Focus.

"Trust me, I've eaten pretty much every single thing on this menu, and I have an opinion about all of it."

"That sounds like a lot of opinions."

"You have no idea."

He liked this waitress and her easy way of talking. He liked her broad smile and her looks. She reminded him of some of the drama club girls he used to pine over when he was young and too scared to talk to anyone female. Thank God those days were behind him.

"Well, what would you recommend?"

"You gotta sweet tooth?"

"I've been known to indulge occasionally."

"Alright then, you gotta try our monster cannoli pancake.

It's delicious. I can't make my way through a whole one by myself, but..." Her eyes narrowed at him. "You look like one of those skinny guys who can just eat and eat and maybe never be satisfied."

"Skinny?" Simon rebuffed. "I haven't been called skinny since I hit puberty." Sure, maybe he tensed the muscles in his forearms to emphasize the point. He wasn't a Sal, or even a Sterling, but his workout schedule in college plus traveling around the entire world largely by foot had left him in some of the best shape of his life. His four-pack had turned somewhere between a six- and an eight-pack depending on the day, and his arms were corded with hard-earned muscle.

But Leilani just eyed him calmly. "Huh, is that so?"

"Why do you say that like you don't believe me."

"Probably because I don't. But who knows, *haoles* have some weird ideas about bodies anyway." She moved right along before he could ask her what a howl-lay was and just how weird those ideas were. "But yeah, you're one of those eaters, I can tell. You'll probably want our Ranchero burger right along with it. Double patty, of course and uh, maybe pepper jack cheese? I think it tastes the best with that and it's not *too* spicy if you have delicate... sensibilities."

It rolled off her tongue with such ease and confidence that he definitely believed her earlier assertion about knowing the entire menu.

"But no milkshake?" he said.

"The cannoli pancake has so much cream and dairy in it that you don't need any of our shakes, but good memory there. Lets me know you're listening."

"How could I not? I'll take exactly what you said, and another beer, if you will."

"Excellent plan," she said with a wink, heading off.

It was only after she disappeared into the door that undoubtedly led to the kitchen that he realized she hadn't written any of it down. Well, he supposed she *had* been the one to suggest the whole meal. Maybe that was just her go-to suggestion that she pulled out on anybody who asked.

But it didn't feel that way, with her smile and her comebacks, it seemed like something she'd recommended just for him. Maybe that was crazy to think, but she definitely had one heck of a service style to have his attention so thoroughly.

With her gone, he tried to get his mind back to his other thoughts, reminiscing about his journey and dreading returning home, but his gaze kept drifting to the kitchen door. The waitress came back with his beer and another quip that had him smiling without realizing it, before disappearing again to serve her other tables.

Naturally, as with most diners, the uncomplicated food came out fast. Simon dug in. Despite all the liquid he'd drank, he *was* hungry, and she had been right about the Miller sons' ability to put it away. The only one who really watched what he ate was Sal, something about macros and proteins and carbs or something.

The monster cannoli pancake really was *monstrous*. The plate was bigger than Simon's head and the ends of the confection hung off the edge of the plate. It was rolled up, like one might expect of the Italian dessert, with a thick tube of delectable cannoli filling right through the center.

It was decadent, it was sinful, and it was oh so *good*.

Leilani rolled around again when his mouth was full of a particularly egregious bite and Simon found himself uncharacteristically flustered. Sure, he wasn't a Casanova by any means, but he'd dated around enough in college, and he certainly hadn't abstained from wooing a beautiful woman in a foreign country. Nothing too torrid, but there were dinners for two in Venice, stolen kisses in the middle of deep forests, embracing and cuddling under stars so much brighter than what was at home.

But none of those women had ever caught him with his cheeks chipmunked out and full of fluffy pancake with cream.

"That good, huh?" she said, smiling in that way that almost made her eyes close.

Simon could only nod, feeling a blush creep up his neck, and by the time he could swallow, she was gone again.

Oh well, it wasn't like the food wasn't plenty to occupy his attention.

He didn't try to rush through his meal, after all, good food should be savored, and he was procrastinating driving the last hour and a half back to the estate, but it was just so tasty that he didn't exactly show much restraint. Before he knew it, both his plates were clean, and he was feeling comfortably stuffed. Sure, he would probably be hungry again in four hours or so, but there was nothing quite like the comforting fullness of his hometown's food.

Leilani came sauntering up later, a glass of water in her hands. She slid it across the table before procuring a straw from within her apron, twirling it artfully around her fingers, before setting it in front of him with a flourish.

"So, how was my recommendation?"

"Spot on, I have to say," Simon said, hand over his stomach, mirroring her earlier reaction. Given all he'd drank and eaten, he was probably down to a two-pack at most. Oh well, Sal would probably be more than happy to walk him through some core workouts. Plus, there was nothing like good old-fashioned riding and summer swimming to keep him strong. "You know what you're talking about."

"I have a habit of that." She took his empty plates just as smoothly. "Anything else I can get you today, friend?"

"I think I'm mighty full this time, but I wouldn't turn down the opportunity to take you out to a place that has a menu I can recommend things from."

Oh.

He hadn't been planning on making a pass at the woman. He had a policy about not bothering women in their places of work. It put an odd pressure on them where they had to balance pleasing a customer and maintaining their own boundaries. And yet he'd just blurted that out without thinking.

"Ain't you sweet? But I'm rather busy most nights, so I'll take a pass. I'll get the check right to you."

It was a kind but firm refusal. Simon forced his expression to stay pleasant and pulled a fifty from his wallet.

"Here, keep the change," he said with a nod before sliding out of the booth.

The woman took a sharp step back as if she was startled, so Simon just offered his hand in a shake. He didn't want her to think he was sore about her "no", but he was a bit embarrassed.

"You've been right lovely. I hope you have a pleasant rest of the day, Miss Leilani."

"And you too, sir. Feel free to come back again if you want any more recommendations."

"I'll keep that in mind."

And with another tip of his head, he was out, heading onto the street and back to his rental.

He didn't resent the pretty waitress, no, not at all, but his pride stung. He hadn't been so quickly and firmly turned down by a woman since... was it his first year of college? Probably. But

Leilani hadn't even seemed remotely taken. Maybe she already had someone?

Maybe, but either way, it just sat sort of weird within Simon.

Oh well. It wasn't like he didn't have other things to worry about.

2

———

Simon

"There you are! My baby is home!"

Simon braced himself just in time for Mom to practically launch herself from the front steps and into his arms. He caught her, swinging her around while the back of his mind wondered if she should be throwing herself around. After all, she had just had a hip replacement.

"Careful there," he said, setting her back down gently. "My brothers would just about kill me if I broke you."

She gave him a look, but it wasn't as terrifying as it was when he was younger. Maybe because he was older, or maybe because she had flour on her nose.

"Like I'd let any of them touch you." She reached up and patted his cheek in a way that was both incredibly maternal but also suffocating.

Simon got that he was the youngest of the bunch. He also

understood that he'd never really been a mama's boy like Sal or the twins or even Samuel. He and his mom had always had a strange relationship, with his mom wanting to hold onto the last of her brood while he wanted to spread his wings.

But he loved her, he really did. He saw how she tried. Maybe if her entire world wasn't built around Dad and what pleased him, she wouldn't be so influenced by him. Wouldn't be caught between four of her older sons and her husband. Maybe she wouldn't have lost Samuel.

Not that Samuel was *dead* or anything, but he'd pretty much cut off most contact with the family after Dad had blown up about his decision to stay with Aunt Annie and Uncle Douglas. Simon never understood why their dad was so mad, considering he never seemed to have liked Samuel and only used him for grunt work, but he guessed it was probably a pride thing.

Ugh. Pride, ranch loyalties, heirs, was that what fueled every decision his family made? It seemed so. If it wasn't so irritating, it might have struck Simon as being... quaint. His little Texas family being so absorbed by Texas life. Did they know there was a whole world out there?

Probably not.

"Mum Miller, you left in an awful hurry and I didn't—Oh! I think I've heard of you."

Simon looked to the door to see a tall woman with striking features and a short pixie cut. That must have been the leggy British woman Sal had texted him about.

"And I've heard of you," he answered, offering his hand. "Nova, right?"

"Hah! Has Sal been talking about me? The big softy. Yeah, I'm Nova, and you must be Simon. The youngest! Was beginning to think you were more of an urban legend than a real Miller boy."

They shared a small laugh, him shaking his head. "Ain't much urban about anything 'round here, I think you'll find."

"Eh, I don't know if that's true anymore since all of us poor folk invaded, isn't it, Mum Miller?"

"As I said before," Mom replied primly, and Simon could tell it was a conversation that the two had had many times. "You can't call it invading if you were invited with open arms."

"Open arms? Is that why Sal tried to get me fired?"

If it weren't for the fact that both of them were grinning, Simon might have been worried. But on the contrary, the two looked pleased as punch and happy to see him. Which was something considering he'd never even met Nova before.

"Go check that the mixer isn't over-beating the meringue while I get my baby situated, please?"

"Baby" wasn't something Simon normally tolerated being called, but he couldn't quite bring himself to object when it came to his mom.

"Sounds like a plan. At least I know now what all this baking furor is over."

Mom shooed Nova off, her cheeks flushed the slightest pink as she turned to face him.

"Baking furor, huh?"

"You shush too! I was excited, alright?"

He couldn't help his chuckle. His mom could be just as sweet as the things that she created. "I'm sure I'll love them, Mom."

"You're right, you will. Now, let me send for a couple of the staff to get your things and you can start to get settled."

"Mom, you know I left most of that behind. I only have a duffle bag and I can carry that myself."

"Only a duffle!" she said with more of a huff than anything else. "I can't imagine my baby wandering around the world with only a single bag to get him by. I sure hope you got that out of your system because *goodness*, I was so worried."

"I was fine, Mom. Really, it was a great experience. You and Dad should maybe try it sometime."

A long shot, and yet he was still disappointed when her nose scrunched up in distaste. "I think I like it plenty right here, actually. But I'll leave you to grabbing your one duffle and washing up." She sent him a look that could only be described as a Mom look. "I trust that you didn't forget how to wash behind your ears out there in the great wilds?"

"No, Mom, I didn't forget."

"Good. Make yourself presentable and then come down for a snack. Your big welcome dinner isn't until tomorrow. Figured you'd like some time to decompress before the festivities start."

"Yeah, because my last dinner went so well."

His mom joshed his arm for that, sending him another look. "As long as you don't have any more *surprise announcements*, we should be good."

Hah, that was one thing to call his declaration that he was going on a six-month backpacking trip that turned into more of a ten-and-a-half-month backpacking trip. Together with all of the prep time that it took to get everything together, his graduation party had been just over a year earlier. Time did love to fly.

"None at the moment, but I'll let you know if I cook anything up."

"You see that you do that. I'm getting on in years, you know, it's not nice to do things like that to an old woman's heart."

"You don't even have gray hair, Mom."

"Well you see, that's because there's this magical place called 'the Salon.'"

"Alright, alright. I get it."

Not a bad welcome home at all. Simon found himself grinning as he grabbed his bag and headed for his wing.

It was the smallest out of all of them, tucked under Sal's, but that had been by choice. He hadn't planned on living his whole life at the estate like the rest of his brothers did, and he thought it was wholly bizarre. Heck, even their cousins up north had their sons make their own family or bachelor cabins on the edges of their sprawling property. And while he wasn't super close with his cousins to the west, he was fairly sure the eldest had her own lil' place a small walk from her parents, and the second eldest was working on one as well. It was only his branch of the family that seemed determined to live on top of each other, and maybe that was where most of their tension came from.

Well, he knew that wasn't true. Their tension came from a lifetime of hunting for approval from a dad who only saw positives in terms of dollar signs.

Simon shook his head. Better not to think about those things. It would put him in a sour mood.

Instead he focused on getting his duffle to his room and pulling things out. Although he did love traveling, it was nice to be back to someplace familiar, even if that familiarity had its own layers of discomfort. And it was even nicer to step into his own shower in his own bathroom. Too many times in his travels the shower head had been lower than him, pointed somewhere around his neck or chest. And that was if he was lucky to get a shower at all. Some of the places he traveled to didn't have running water.

And yet they seemed happier than him. Had they found some secret of contentment—or was that the payoff for living in a small world? He didn't know. He didn't think he ever would.

He was feeling warm, clean and refreshed when he stepped out of the shower and started to get changed. He was sure his mom would have his wardrobe filled in no time with new clothes for around the ranch.

But it wasn't until he was fully dressed and ready to head down the stairs that a strange feeling slid along the back of his mind, slowly pushing itself to the forefront like a creeping vine. And it was in the middle of his almost empty room, in the uncharacteristic silence, that he realized what was off.

The place just felt so *empty*.

Sure, Sterling had used a couple of rooms in his wing for when he needed space from Silas. And Mom had told him she was converting the room closest to the garage as a sort of crafting area, where she could work on presents without worrying about anyone walking in on her and ruining the surprise. But other than that, it was still.

Unused.

Unnecessary.

That feeling suddenly magnified, rolling bitter and virulent down his tongue. The quiet, the stillness of it, the sort of manicured clean that the staff had probably been doing in the years he'd been at college, all of it reminded him of the complete lack of *anything* he had to do.

No job, no hobbies, no real passions. He loved learning, he loved experiencing new things, but someone couldn't build their whole life out of it. There needed to be depth to it—a meaning.

And Simon wasn't sure there'd ever been a time where he'd felt so completely without passion.

Ugh.

Shaking his head, he forced himself to keep moving. Maybe if he found things to do, the restlessness wouldn't make him feel like he was going to sink into the quicksand. For once, he wouldn't mind a little bit of pomp and circumstance to distract him. At least being annoyed was better than the listless feeling in his chest.

But true to her word, Mom didn't make a big to-do of his first night home. No one did. Sal came in and gave him a big ol' hug before disappearing somewhere with Nova—something about a star picnic—and then Sterling came in, clapped him on the back, and said he looked well.

Silas and Solomon never arrived. When Simon asked, Mom said they were grown men and she didn't keep track of their whereabouts. Which was, uh, interesting to say the least. But Simon just tucked that away and enjoyed eating the snacks his mom had made and watching her finish up the last of her baking.

It was a nice time. He heard more about his brothers and the rather insane stories of how each of them met their new ladies. It was insane to think that he was suddenly the only single child in the family. While his brothers had dated plenty when they were younger, the demands of helping grow an empire and Sterling's rather infamous actions with two wealthy sisters had them tapering off their dating life once they were done with college. In fact, Simon hadn't heard about any of his brothers dating anyone since he was a senior in high school, and suddenly, all of them were either engaged or very seriously dating.

Wild.

While Simon loved women, the beauty of them, the curve of them, the lilt of their voices and the gentleness which they treated those they trusted, he'd never once felt compelled to wrap up his whole life in one. People were nice, and sure, people could even be amazing. But it just felt like so... *much*.

He didn't say that, of course. Just nodded and smiled and enjoyed his mom's animated talking. He did love seeing her so full of life. Sometimes, especially after her hip surgery, she seemed so exhausted just by getting through the day. It used to be the only places he saw her smile was her garden and her chicken coop.

Things had changed on the ranch and in the estate, alright, but none of that filled the void that felt like it was gaping in his chest.

So, when Mom bid him goodnight and kissed him on the cheek, softly saying she was so glad that he was home, he went to his room. But that lasted maybe all of ten minutes before he was pacing again, unable to rest.

He found his hand on his phone again, texting up several of his old school friends, the very ones he had thought about earlier. Surely if anyone was up and about, it would be them.

Thankfully, four of them answered and before Simon could really debate about it, he was out in his rental and driving toward town. Maybe he drove faster than he should have, maybe he didn't, but it was exhilarating to be behind the wheel of a powerful truck again. As a result, he arrived about fifteen minutes earlier than he should have.

Which was a mistake. He *hated* being still.

His whole journey across the world was supposed to fix that, wasn't it? And yet he was still just as antsy, just as unfulfilled as he'd been when he left. Maybe he just needed to have fun?

Yeah, fun was good.

At least most of his friends were fairly punctual, and soon all four of them rolled up in their various cars, paid for their parking, then they were on their way to have a real night on the town.

There was a flicker of warmth within him as they started out, one that grew as they joked about old times and exaggerated capers they had gotten into. Simon had been to hundreds of nights on the town all across the world, from ritzy, guided experiences to just drinking homemade mead or moonshine while sitting on a dirt floor, but nothing quite beat being home.

Even if it was a fleeting sort of feeling, Simon chased it. He made sure not to drink too much, but he definitely had a full beer at every bar they stopped into, enough to make his belly warm and his shoulders relax. Finally, he felt more carefree, a bit less encumbered by the gaping chasm that always seemed to be just under his feet.

Eventually they ended up at Josiah's favorite dive bar. Simon had never understood it when he was younger, but now he understood that it was one of the few bars around town that would regularly let eighteen- and nineteen-year-olds come in on Friday night until midnight and play at both the pool tables and the pinball machines. Funny, how he'd never thought of that back then.

Simpler times.

"Alright, I'll rack 'em up!" Josiah called almost as soon as they were in the door, beelining for what Simon assumed was his favorite table. He went along amiably, before splitting off to order some more drinks.

After that the minutes started to quickly slide into each other, blending with the comforting sound of pool balls hitting their targets, the cool beer and the reminiscing about old times. It had been just what Simon needed, even if he knew he would be back to feeling just as directionless in the morning. He supposed he could get completely smashed and that could buy him some more time, but he'd never been one to purposefully get drunk. He liked his beer, he liked his homebrewed stuff, but all in all, he hated feeling either dumbed-down or powerless, both of which came hand in hand with going over his personal limit.

So no, getting drunk wasn't an option. But at least being slightly tipsy was on the table. Just enough to make him smile a little easier and feel less like a boat adrift in a world-covering sea.

"Hey, Simon, you wanna treat us to another round of drinks?" his buddy Thaddeus asked with a wink.

If it had been anybody else, it would have been rude, but Thad knew how much Simon liked to treat his friends out. In fact, if he could make a career out of giving the guys amazing nights out, then he would. Because at least that was something that gave him some satisfaction.

"Y'all are some moochers," he countered sarcastically while waving at the bartender and making the international symbol for another round. The burly man gave a nod and then that was that. "You're lucky I like y'all."

"How could you not?" Josiah said, batting his eyes. "I'm patently adorable."

"Yeah, your wifey tell you that?" James countered with a huff of a laugh.

"No, my wifey calls me her big strong manly man. My *mom* calls me adorable."

That got another round of mirth in their little group. They could all tease each other like that, in the knowing way that only friends of many years had. He liked it, and he realized that he had missed it.

Maybe that was what he needed? More meaningful connections? Sure, he had friends in every port and people seemed to like him wherever he went. But how many people was he *close* to? Not many. He didn't exactly trust easily.

But maybe that was also a question to deal with when he wasn't tipsy and having a good time.

"I've got a pitcher of cold beer here, two of our imported dark lagers and a hard cider?"

Simon looked away from his friends to thank the server, and he knew he definitely needed to ease up on the drinks because it took his mind several seconds to realize that voice was *very* familiar. Blinking, he realized it was none other than the waitress from the diner standing there with a tray full of their drinks.

Wait... what? They weren't at the diner, were they?

No. He wasn't *that* drunk.

He smiled at her, about to say her name, but she seemed to take his nodding grin as an answer to whether the drinks were his or not, and started to set them down on the tall table next to him.

"Are you having a good game?" she said, friendly smile back on her round face. Was she wearing makeup? She hadn't been in the diner, but her eyes looked even brighter and her lips were a ruby red.

"They are," he said, unable to tell if she recognized him or not. "I'm just watching."

"Not a man of action, or just not a man of billiards?"

"Billiards," he confirmed, taking one of the beers and screwing the top off with his hand.

"Yikes, that always hurts my palms whenever I try." She held up the limb, her fingers wiggling. Her palm looked so soft that he had the strange urge to press his face into it.

Whoa there, Simon. That was weird, even to his tipsy self. He should probably drink this next beer slowly.

"Anyway, you have a good night. Just wave down Clint if you need another round."

And then she was gone, sashaying back to the bar where another lot of drinks was already waiting for her to pick up.

Had she recognized him? It seemed like no, but it also seemed like yes. She was probably just that friendly with everybody, and she saw dozens of people a day, so he knew logically that there was no reason for her to remember him.

But still, his pride smarted. People always remembered him. He was *memorable*. People didn't just *forget* him.

And yet he stood there, sipping his beer, clearly forgotten. Either she didn't remember him or she was pretending not to. He wasn't sure which he would prefer because both had plenty of downsides. It would be best if he could just forget it and leave it be. She'd probably had far too many people ask her out and then be awkward about it the next time she saw them. Who could blame her for pretending they'd never seen each other before?

Or at least that was what he told himself, but over the next half hour, he found himself making excuses to visit the bar or walk by it more than he normally would. Nothing excessive, of course, but after several cruises by, he was more hydrated than he usually would be. At least future Simon would thank him for all the cups of water he sipped at until he was sober enough for his next drink.

Unfortunately, all that water had to go somewhere, and nearly an hour after their arrival, he told his friends he had to hit the bathroom. They all teased him for being the first one to have to go—but his bladder didn't give two snakes about their teasing.

Unlike the women's room, there wasn't a line. Simon was able to go in and out, and he was grateful Josiah's favorite place didn't have disgusting bathrooms. He'd had to use literal holes in the ground during his travels, but that certainly didn't mean he preferred less than tidy restrooms.

But as he exited, he paused for a second to adjust the rolled sleeves of his shirt. Although really it was just an excuse to scope out where Leilani was. Serving, of course, as was her job. He wasn't sure why he was so hung up on one woman, but that question froze in his head as the patron she was serving took a full handful of her backside and pulled her up against him.

No.

That was *not* alright.

Sure, Simon was a little tipsy, but one didn't manhandle *anyone* ever without their permission, and one certainly didn't put their hands on a hard-working lady in the middle of her job.

It was like something else took over him. He stood straighter, his mind cleared, and a beat later he was striding toward them, fire burning in his brain. He only made it one step, maybe two, before Leilani wrenched herself away then suddenly socked the guy right in the face.

Her form seemed good enough, especially considering that the large man went tumbling off his stool, but Simon wasn't particularly concerned with her posture.

No, mostly his brain was caught somewhere between still needing to fight and protect and also needing to digest what might have just been the hottest thing he'd ever seen.

"Don't you dare touch me!" Leilani practically snarled, her teeth bared in her profile and her posture tense.

Simon wouldn't have been surprised if thunder clapped overhead, even Mother Nature herself needing to recognize the force that was standing in the mortal bar.

There was a faint beat of quiet, where everyone seemed to be catching up with what happened.

And then the trouble started.

The guy's friends all started yelling, one helping him up but most trying to crowd Leilani. The tall woman just squared her shoulders and pulled up her fists, for all the world looking like she was willing to take on every one of them without breaking a sweat.

And for all Simon knew, she probably could. The smiley, charming and rounded woman was gone, leaving someone else entirely right in her spot. Someone strong. Someone who looked like she was more than happy to sock the man again.

"Hey, hey, hey!" That was probably from the bartender behind the counter. His voice was moving as if he was running toward the fray, but Simon's body kicked into gear too. He strode forward, gripping the shoulder of one of the louder men and pulling him back.

"Why don't you settle down?" he asked, using his best authoritative voice. It was modeled after his father before he had started to lose his temper all the time, and it seemed to work because the man blinked at him a moment.

"You work here?"

"No, but I saw your friend there put his hands on a lady. We don't take to that around here."

"Bull. He's got a wife; he ain't done nothing."

"Think whatever you want, but think it outside where all of you have a chance to calm down."

"He didn't do anything!"

Simon could faintly hear others in the background yelling something about cops, and there were definitely a couple of people on their phones. That probably wasn't good.

"I saw otherwise."

"Then you saw wrong. Craig's wife is a Grade-A fox. Why would he waste his time on some fat, illegal bar girl?"

Simon was going to have to rethink the idea that he didn't really have a temper, because suddenly it burst out hot and virulent from inside of him. He brought up his own hands, barely catching himself at the last moment.

Or maybe he didn't so much "catch" himself as one of his drunken buddies suddenly stumbled into his back. The man who'd been arguing turned away, giving Simon a moment to stand back and breathe.

"Whoa, what's happening over here?" Josiah said, pool cue still in hand.

"Some guy put hands on one of the employees," Simon said tersely.

Where was Leilani? Where was the bartender? For that matter, where was the handsy guy? Were they already outside? Simon tried to crane his neck to see, but it seemed like the whole bar had erupted into a hubbub between people pointing fingers, taking pictures, arguing and recording the whole incident.

"You know, this doesn't really make for a good night. Why don't we get out of here?" Another one of his friends asked, eyeing the place with discomfort. Simon didn't blame him. Alex had always been twitchy as a kid—something called anxiety now—and he didn't always do well with loud noises or angry yelling, both of which were happening all around him.

"Yeah, let's go."

Thankfully, it wasn't winter, so they didn't have to worry about coats or anything like that. They took the last swigs of their drinks then headed out. But as soon as they were on the other side of the door, it became very apparent just where the folks in question had gone off to. Turned out someone *had* called the cops, and there was already a squad car outside, one officer talking to the handsy man and his group, the other talking to the bartender and Leilani.

She looked upset. That wasn't good. In fact, it was so not good that it made the last of the warms Simon had felt from his beer fizzle right up out of him. Of course, she had every right to be upset; he just hated the idea that she *was.*

It wasn't like him to nose in other people's business, but he found himself rooted to the spot. Was she okay? Was she angry? Was she hurt? Had that guy said anything to her? If he had, Simon was going to call up one of his family's lawyers and have them tie the man up in litigation so high that his grand-children felt it. Maybe tell his wife how he liked to treat service people as well.

"Hey, man, you coming?"

Thad's call pulled him out of the growing tirade in his head. Why was he getting so worked up about someone he'd met once? Yeah, he'd always been about justice and fairness, and he *hated* bullies, but Leilani had already turned him down; what if she thought it was creepy that he ended up at the bar she worked at and stuck around? *He* knew it wasn't intentional, but she would have no way of knowing. And considering how insane some people were, he couldn't exactly blame her for being suspicious.

Ugh. It was all messy.

"I think I'm going to call it a night and get back home. My mom has a bunch of stuff planned to welcome me back tomorrow."

"Aw, are you sure?" Josiah asked with only a hint of a whine. "We haven't seen you in *ages.*"

"I promise I'll be around a lot more often. We can do this again next week sometime."

"Only if you promise," Thad said in that inexplicably dry

way of speaking that made it impossible to tell if he was being sarcastic or not. He had a gift. "And you don't leave us again for a shiny new diploma."

"No more diplomas. At least for a while."

They all shared a laugh at the second part of his concession and then they meandered off, no doubt to make their way to another dive bar that was someone else's favorite.

Simon watched them go, pulling his phone out and trying to look like he was ordering a ride and not that he was lingering for the drama. He didn't care about that; he just wanted to make sure Leilani was okay.

And maybe he also wanted a good look at the grabber's face. Whenever his mind replayed the image for him, he could see the man's long, tanned fingers as they bit into the seat of her jeans. It hadn't been a pat, or even a playful spank—not that either of those would have been appropriate either—but it was something *mean*, something meant to hurt and maybe even leave her with fingerprints to remember him by.

So yeah, maybe he was being foolish by wanting to check on her, but he couldn't help it. She had been nice to him, soothed him on a day that he was full of worry and dread. And maybe, just maybe, it was because in those couple of moments where he was striding forward to defend her, he hadn't felt directionless at all.

It took at least another twenty minutes before the cops cleared, escorting the man and his friends away but not arresting them. In fact, there wasn't a handcuff in sight. The bartender said a couple of things to Leilani that Simon couldn't hear before returning inside, leaving only the server standing outside.

Simon approached her cautiously. The last thing he wanted to do was startle her, and her mind definitely seemed to be other places. She stood there silently, a stony expression on her face, her breathing measured.

"You alright?" he asked as gently as he could. And he was grateful when she didn't jump or startle, her head simply turning to his with a slow sort of resignation.

"I am."

"The cops give you a hard time?"

She shook her head. "No, thank goodness. Maybe it would be a different story if it wasn't self-defense, but they're not taking any sort of report."

"That's good then." Wait, was it? The guy who grabbed her was just getting to walk away? That wasn't right.

"Yeah. *That's* good."

Her tone indicated that something else very much *wasn't* good, and he got the sense that it was not the opportune moment to try to get her number. Not that he had been going to ask, considering she already turned him down, but he'd *thought* about it.

"So, are they giving you the night off or do you have to finish out your shift?"

"Oh, something like that."

"Pardon?"

Her eyes met his and she let out a sigh. "I've been fired. There's a strict no violence policy except for the bouncers and the bartender. Apparently, it's an insurance issue."

"But... there are no bouncers." That was one of the reasons Josiah had loved the bar.

"I'm aware of that," she said dryly. Her accent came in thicker when she was upset, but he still couldn't place it. It lingered on the edge of his brain, just barely familiar. "And of course the owner of the bar is also the owner of the diner I work at, that was how I even got this gig in the first place, so I'm fired there too. I just went from two jobs to unemployed because some *haole* wanted to get handsy. Sometimes I hate the mainland!"

There was plenty of anger in the last sentence, but all Simon could do was blink at her. She had been *fired*?! What! He was probably still tipsy, but he was sure that even sober that wouldn't make any sense to him. How did they fire a woman for defending herself? *Insurance reasons*? Sounded highly suspect to him.

His mind was so whirring with righteous indignation and wondering if he could find the name of both the owner and the grabber, that his mouth moved entirely of its own volition. Not something it did very often, but alcohol certainly helped it run its own motor.

"I can give you a job."

3

Leilani

*A*pparently, Leilani was suddenly a ranch worker.

That was the thought that made her head spin several times as a tall woman named Nova walked her around the truly massive spread of land that belonged to the famous Miller family. But only one of the locations. She'd read that there were actually five Miller ranches total and one affiliate dairy and organic produce farm.

There was the one slightly up north in Montana, one to the west in New Mexico, and the main one she was on now. The one in Montana was the "renowned" one that she'd learned had been in their family for generations and was how they became ridiculously wealthy. The western one was only two generations old and was taken over by one of the Miller brothers from a great aunt that had never married. Then there was a very small one in Iowa that was more for processing and run by a cousin of a cousin or something, one up in Washington that was also small and self-sufficient, only, not a business like the others.

And finally, was the big ol' farm that was almost as old as the Montana ranch, created when one of their adopted workers came into money and moved there with his mail-order bride. There was actually a great story there, but Leilani reminded herself that she needed to concentrate on the info-dump that the British woman was giving her.

The last thing she wanted to do was seem ungrateful. Especially since she potentially had a situation that could set her up financially in a way her waitressing job never could have.

It wasn't like she was a vet or a vet tech, like either of the tall women she had met. And she wasn't one of the regular workers trained on all the automation and equipment or upkeep. She was basically useless, and yet... she was suddenly working fewer hours and making *more* money. Basically, about three dollars an hour more, even compared to her best nights at waitressing.

And it was *regular* pay too. Not tip-dependent work that revolved around the holidays or whether she was given enough of the rush shifts. She wished that legislation would come through that would give servers minimum wage and do away with tipping, but she knew most folks didn't think twice about service workers. And even if they did, they would just tell her to "get a job," as if good jobs just grew on trees and were easy to come by.

And working here, she wasn't going to have to worry about patrons dumping beer on her, or someone trying to steal tips from a server, or someone pretending there was hair in their food to get some sort of refund. And judging by how the man who had offered her a job had acted, she wouldn't have to deal with being manhandled either.

"So over here you see we have the cat shelters. They're small bins, I know, but it works real well for them with hay inside. The important part is to make sure you don't approach them directly. Let them come to you at first. It'll take a while to earn their trust, but it'll be worth it."

Leilani couldn't believe it. Part of her job was playing with cats?

"You have a look on your face," Nova said with a laugh. "Am I going too fast? I heard I can be kind of overwhelming when I get going."

"No, you're fine," Leilani said with a smile. She liked this Nova person, with her interesting accent and fun phrases that Leilani had only ever heard on the TV. "I just can't believe I landed this. I'm not this lucky, if you know what I mean."

"Oh man, do I. Used to think I was cursed or something."

"What changed?"

"Honestly, this place. If Elizabeth hadn't hired me, I'd probably still be cramped in my tiny apartment that I could barely afford with a car that was falling apart."

"So they really are good employers?"

"Yeah, thanks to a lot of work from the brothers, the opportunities here are amazing."

"And all this for just cleaning animal stalls and playing with cats?"

"Well, muckraking is very physically demanding. Then we'll also need you to play and interact with the pigs. You'll also be picking up the feral cats that have been caught in Elizabeth's traps for her catch and release program."

"Catch and release?"

"Yeah. Feral cats can help with pests on farms, ranches and

in the city, but they can also wipe out local eco-systems. Compromise on that is capturing cats, fixing them so they can't get female cats pregnant, then releasing them back into the wild."

"Wow, and that works?"

"Seems to so far. And don't forget handling the baby goats to get them real used to humans. And for the calves, brushing, patting their heads, scratching behind their ears. Even playing games with them."

"Yeah, you say all that like it's hard."

"Not hard, but certainly exhausting. Sterling and Elizabeth have added goats just four months ago. And now they're expanding on their breeding program to enrich the calves' lives, so it's important to be flexible."

Leilani nodded emphatically. She was happy to go home thoroughly exhausted if it meant she would be earning eighteen dollars an hour plus insurance and benefits. She was going to have time off! *Paid* time off! She might even have a way to visit her mother and siblings.

And oh *man*, was her mom going to cry the next time Leilani sent her money. It would probably be enough for Ori to get another pair of shoes before the sports season kicked in. Goodness knew her kid brother was growing like a weed. She had no doubt that soon he'd be taller than her by several inches.

Personally, she suspected maybe a lil' Samoan snuck into their family line, but her mother swore up and down they were straight Hawaiian until her *haole* grandfather had met her *kanaka Maoli* grandmother and sparks had flown. A mix of French, German and Filipino, it was his light eyes that she'd inherited while her youngest sister had his paler complexion and a light dusting of freckles.

"So, do you have any questions? I've been monologuing at you for about two hours now, and I could use a water myself."

Leilani followed her into what looked like a mechanic's garage, where the tall woman led her to a mini fridge that was well stocked with water and sports drinks. Along with…

"Is that aloe gel?" she asked, pointing to the large bottle that was on its side.

"Yeah, it's for all us white folks that tend to burn up," Nova said with a laugh. "Especially Teddy. Although, Frenchie has been using it too when she forgets to put her sunscreen on when gardening. I've got a feeling that she's still getting used to being able to just *buy* things to take care of herself even if it's been a couple of years."

Leilani paused mid-drink. There was a lot of information in a very short space, but most of it was her eyes locked onto the woman and her olive skin and dark features. "You're not mixed?"

Another laugh from her, but it wasn't mean. "Nope, Caucasian through and through. Don't worry about it. I'm well aware of how ethnically ambiguous I look. What did you think I was?"

"Honestly, mixed Middle Eastern and European. I have several friends back home that look similar to you that have that heritage."

"Oh really?" She smiled amiably and Leilani decided she liked this Nova lady. "That's cool! Where's home then, I'm from the UK, somewhat obviously."

"Hawaii. Oahu specifically."

"Oahu? That's where the capital is, right? Honolulu? And that one pink hospital, right?"

Leilani's eyes went wide again. "You know about Hawaii?"

"No, not really. Just army stuff from being a military brat.

When I lived in Guam, I had some friends who mentioned they were born in that pink hospital."

"But... those are American bases."

"Yup. I'm American."

"You're American, but you're from the UK and you lived in Guam?"

"Yup. Fun stuff. Anyway, questions?"

"How tall are you?" It was out of left field, sure, but Leilani wasn't used to meeting women who were taller than her, especially by several inches.

"Somewhere between six foot and six foot one, depending on who you ask. I'm about the same height as Elizabeth. Why do you ask?"

"Just curious. It's not often I meet a pair of mainlanders who are both three inches taller than me."

"I know what you mean! I'm used to being the tallest, but I don't even stand out around here. It's pretty nice, actually. Almost makes me feel normal."

"Ew, who wants to feel normal?"

Nova chuckled at that before draining the rest of her water bottle. "Yeah, I knew we were going to get along. If you don't have any other questions right now, we should ship you off to Silas and get that onboarding paperwork done."

"Ah, paperwork. My favorite thing ever."

"I hear that, but Silas makes it a little less awful. Or at least expedient. Maybe that's the same thing. Ready?"

"Ready."

Leilani followed her out to a golf cart and to a truly massive mansion. Instantly Leilani felt small and out of place, but Nova continued on like there was nothing to be concerned about.

The house was exceptionally beautiful on the inside too, with meticulously carved crown molding and beautifully curved stairs up to a second floor. The furniture all looked expensive and there were beautiful indoor plants in several places, balanced perfectly to make things welcoming without being crowded.

She didn't have much time to gawk before she was let into what looked like a personal office where a handsome man was sitting behind a desk, typing away at his computer. He definitely had similar features to the man who'd offered her a job, strong jaw and broad shoulders, but his hair had more of a curl to it and was more of a chestnut brown instead of the deep, dark brown of the stranger she'd met.

What was his name? She should really remember the guy who potentially turned her life around. At first she'd been sure he'd be one of those annoying rich guys who thought that he was God's gift to the earth, but after he'd offered her a job and hadn't tried to come on to her or flirt with her further, she'd decided to be grateful to him instead of suspicious.

"Oh, hello there. You must be the worker my little brother told me about. I'm Silas."

Ah, Silas. She'd read about him a little. There wasn't a lot of information out beyond Solomon, Sterling, Sal and Simon, but she remembered reading that he was the older, less notorious twin. Sterling, the younger one, had made waves when he dated two sisters from a rich family. Apparently, he'd settled down since then, but that had been a wild read.

"Leilani. Leilani Cunningham."

"Right, Ms. Cunningham. I've been getting things ready while Nova was giving you the grand tour, so hopefully this will go quickly."

"What, you want to get rid of me already?" Leilani asked with what she called her patent dazzle-smile.

And just as she hoped, Silas let out a short laugh. "Hardly.

But I do have a dinner to make in the city and if I'm late, I'd hate to think of what my fiancée might do to my food if she's bored."

"She's a red-head," Nova said in a false stage whisper, winking before leaving out the door.

"I'm going to tell her you said that!" Silas called after her, but Nova was already gone. "Well," Silas said, returning his gaze to her. "Shall we get started?"

LEILANI HOPPED into her junker of a car, practically vibrating and wanting to pinch herself all over. They'd finished up the paperwork just as quickly as Nova had alluded, and she was being let go early *with* full pay. She couldn't believe it. And she was going to be paid weekly, so she definitely was going to get a fat, juicy paycheck before rent was due again. She was so excited.

As soon as she was on the road, she pulled to the side and whipped out her cellphone, texting her auntie to see if she needed to be picked up. She didn't have to wait too long for an answer, which confirmed her auntie could definitely use a ride.

Leilani smiled to herself and took to the road again, pretty sure she knew the way to the physical therapy building that her auntie used. Since she was getting a check before big bills rolled in, she could afford to treat the older woman out.

Which, to be frank, she absolutely deserved. A lot of times Leilani felt guilty by how much she'd had to lean on her auntie ever since she'd come to the mainland, and a single dinner was the least she could do. Auntie Kini wasn't technically her immediate aunt, more like her grandma's sister, but on the islands you called older women "auntie" as a sign of respect and affection.

Leilani's plans might have grown more elaborate after the hour and forty minutes it took to get to the building, where of course her auntie was already waiting outside. That was another thing that Leilani could always count on her for, timeliness. Which showed her consideration for others.

"Hey there, Auntie!" Leilani said, pulling up to the curb and unlocking her door. "Did you have a good day at physical therapy?"

"Goodness, they put me through my paces, I tell you! I'm ready to go home."

"Really?" Leilani asked casually. "You're not hungry after all that work?"

"Oh, I am, but I have some cold cuts at home and rice in my cooker, so we can have snacks as soon as we're there."

"Actually, I was thinking of taking you out to dinner."

"Dinner? *Mea aloha*, you don't have to do that. I have food at home."

"I know, but I've got some money coming in and there's a mid-week special at that sushi place we've been eying."

"...sushi?"

Leilani didn't miss the way her auntie perked up at that. "Yeah. But, I mean, if you're not interested—"

"No, no, I'm fine. If you want to treat me, I won't complain. It's been forever since I've had sushi."

"Alright! Sounds like a plan."

Plugging the name of the restaurant into her GPS, Leilani had a hard time not bouncing in her seat as she drove. Her auntie was right; it had been ages since they'd gone out to eat. Between some expensive repairs for her car and braces on her younger sister Malia, she, her auntie, and her mom were all pretty strapped.

And even if she knew the sushi wouldn't be as good as at home on the island—that was just physically impossible—she knew it would be good enough to at least be tasty. And after the amazing day she'd had, capping it off with some yummy fish, rice and *nori* seemed like an excellent idea.

They arrived with an hour left to go on the special and Leilani swore they almost ran in. She was happy when they were seated quickly and before too long, she had unagi and a spicy salmon roll in front of her while her auntie had a rainbow roll and some red tuna maki.

"So, what is this money you've come into? You're not suddenly selling drugs, are you?"

It was a joke, but Leilani gave her auntie a look anyway. "No, it's not drugs. I got a new job, actually."

"Oh, and you just found out about it today? And that's why your poor auntie hasn't heard a word about it since you lost your jobs last Friday?"

"Well, no, I was offered it on Friday about two minutes after I was fired. But you know how things are, Auntie. I wanted to make sure that it was legit."

"And this meal means I can assume it's legit?"

"Through and through. I'm a ranch hand now, for real."

"A ranch hand?" The older woman clapped with delight. "Now you have to tell me exactly how *that* unfolded."

Leilani did, only leaving out the part where she met the man who hired her at the diner and how he'd asked her out. She still wasn't one hundred percent sure that was what he had been doing. He might have just been an oblivious rich guy who wanted to show off his favorite restaurant—but she figured it hadn't been worth the risk and turned him down. Unlike most, however, he'd taken it graciously and hadn't seemed ruffled in the slightest. Strange, but definitely not an unwelcome development.

They ended up staying long past the hour of the special, although they didn't eat anything else. Leilani *did*, however, insist on treating her auntie to one of their small glasses of *sake*. A Japanese liquor, it was something the older woman had reminisced about from time to time when she got to talking about her adventures back on the Hawaiian islands, and it made Leilani feel warm and happy inside to watch the woman sip at her drink and smile. She might have tried it herself if she hadn't sworn off alcohol after a disastrous first time drinking back when she was nineteen. Maybe she would try it again someday, but usually it just reminded her of things she very much wanted to forget.

Funny, she loved listening to her auntie remember her past, but she mostly wished she could forget all of hers.

No, forgetting was the wrong word. She wanted to *erase* it. Wipe it all away like it wasn't there.

Too bad life didn't work that way.

But she refused to let such thoughts ruin an excellent dinner with her auntie, especially since it was the first one in ages. So, she packed up those thoughts and fears that were trying to slip in and shoved them to the back of her mind. It was easier than it had been when she first left the islands, but she didn't know if that was a good thing.

"Thank you so much for treating me out," her auntie said once Leilani dropped her off in front of her small home just between the nicer side of the city and the slums. "You know, all that good food has made me sleepy. You sure you don't want to come in and spend the night in my guest room?"

"Aw, Auntie, you know I have my own place."

"I know, I know. But can I help it if I miss you? This house is too big with just me in it."

That was most certainly not true. Leilani had lived in that house for almost a year and it was incredibly cramped, especially with the two of them in there. That combined with feeling like a burden had Leilani save up and get a second job so she could afford her own studio about five minutes away. Sure, that was cramped too, but at least she wasn't driving up her auntie's bills and taking up her limited space.

"I have a steady schedule now, so we'll be able to hang out more often."

"Oh yes, I forgot. You mentioned that. Monday through Friday. That'll be quite the change."

"Yeah, it will. I'll be like a regular working person."

"Goodness, I'm not sure if either of us will be able to handle that."

"You're telling me," Leilani said as her auntie laughed, then slowly shuffled to get out of the car. Although she'd hid it well during their dinner and lengthy talk, it was clear that the older woman was indeed sore from her physical therapy. "Do me a favor and take a bath with some Epsom salts, okay?"

"*Mea aloha*, you don't know me at all if you don't think I already have a long-standing date with my tub."

"Hah! That's my Auntie!" She blew a kiss and made sure to watch all the way until the older woman was inside before driving off. And for the first time in a very long while, she was feeling hopeful about the future.

4

Simon

That Leilani girl was something else.

And not in a bad way! A very good way... a very good but *frustrating* way and Simon had to remind himself that he wasn't supposed to be spending several hours puzzling over an employee. Especially an employee that he himself hired.

And yet, he was watching her out of the corner of his eye as she worked, slowly introducing herself to some of the more outgoing pigs in the outside pen. He was supposed to be helping Silas re-dig some fence posts that had been damaged in a big storm a year and a half earlier, then further damaged after what was basically a tornado swept through. Simon didn't understand why his brother was doing the kind of work they usually payed someone else to do. Not that he minded getting dirty, and he certainly didn't mind using his hands. But he figured while they were working, he could also spend some time people-watching.

And mostly he meant Leilani-watching.

He knew she was friendly, but it was really amazing how she fit right in with the other women of the ranch. Granted, he was only observing from afar, but it really seemed like she just clicked instantly. He'd thought maybe it would have been harder for her to integrate into their operation considering his family's status. That and the shock and awe of hanging with the rich and demi-famous of Texas elite, but she didn't seem to pay him or his brother any mind.

Granted, it had only been a week. There was a chance that she didn't realize that she was interacting with *the* Miller brothers of Texas. Literally a clan of the hottest and wealthiest bachelors—well, actually, he guessed he was the only bachelor now. All of his brothers had found someone and were either engaged or seemed to be getting close to it.

Strange.

It wasn't that he was jealous. He didn't crave a relationship or need some woman to put him through a spiritual or life revelation. He was fine the way he was. But it was rather... grating that all of them had done some sort of 180 or great improvement after meeting someone from Dallas or the surrounding area, none of them going farther than their back-yards for a partner.

Well, except for maybe Nova who seemed to be... British, maybe? He was vaguely aware that there was some sort of detail he was missing, but she still didn't count either because she'd been living in America for a while before Sal ran into her.

Literally, from what Simon had heard.

"You know, you can stop staring and just go talk to her."

Simon practically burst through the roof of his truck; he'd

jumped so hard. And that would be a real shame considering he'd turned his rental in a couple of days earlier when his new ride had been delivered.

"Don't startle me like that, man. I'm getting to be old like you."

"You're hilarious," Silas countered with a deadpan. "Mid-twenties and you're still telling old jokes."

"I'll stop as soon as they stop being funny."

"Uh-huh, I imagine they're usually pretty good at changing the subject too, but I'm the King of Avoidance, and trust me when I say it'll do you a whole lotta good to just go talk to her."

"I have no idea what you're talking about."

"Look, three of your five brothers ended up going out with an employee that we hired, so the trend is working out so far. Not to mention ol' Samuel is getting hitched to a worker on our aunt and uncle's ranch. At this rate, you'd be possibly missing a great opportunity if you didn't reach out."

"I just want to see how the new worker is settling in. She's the first person I ever hired, you know. I don't need to *talk* to her."

"You know, I might almost believe you if I didn't have almost this exact same conversation with Sterling about Elizabeth."

Now *that* surprised Simon. "Really?"

"Yeah. Really. All I'm saying is it can't hurt to try it, right?"

Oh, it could hurt alright. He'd already been turned down once. And asking a woman out after providing her a job seemed... murky at best. What if she thought he only gave her the job in return for... *favors*? That was the absolute last thing he wanted, and the thought made his stomach churn.

But he wasn't as naïve as his brothers. He'd been around the world and had seen things. He knew the kind of trials and tribulations women went through. Add on top of that, Leilani was young, a woman of color and *poor*, and well, that sure was a situation that made it easy to be taken advantage of.

"It definitely can," Simon grumbled, taking his car out of park. His brother got the message and stepped back, hands up in a placating way. But Simon didn't want to be placated. He wanted to feel like he *belonged*, like he had a purpose, as easily as it seemed Leilani did.

"Okay, you have a point. But think about it, alright?"

Simon absolutely wouldn't. He didn't say as much, of course, knowing it would be dismissed as youngest brother stubbornness, so he just drove back home. Silas could handle the fence posts by himself and if Sterling was around, well the twins would probably just finish the job together.

Maybe it would all be different if Simon was the one with a twin. Maybe, but that was like wishing on fishes: easy to do but not very productive. As it were, he was a man adrift amongst about a dozen people who all somehow seemed to have found some chunk of land to cling to.

None of it made sense.

He wasn't sure what he was planning to do when he got back to the manor, probably just mess around on his computer while he brainstormed things to occupy himself. But nowhere in his plans did it involve his dad standing at the top of the stairs.

"Come with me," he said flatly, turning around on his heel and disappearing past where Simon could see.

For a moment he thought about disobeying his father. It was no secret that he hadn't always been in line like all of his brothers. While they had tried for years to be the perfect sons, Simon had always run along the border of what would be allowed. But his trip around the world had certainly pushed that marker, and Simon was under no illusion that he wasn't on his father's bad-side list. He never wanted to be in outright rebellion and possibly risk his inheritance and comfortable lifestyle, but he also liked seeing how far he could go.

It seemed like the perfect time to do just that, so he went up the stairs and followed his dad to his study.

The room was still as intimidating as he remembered it. It had no right to be considering the good lighting and high, reaching windows with complementary, silk curtains, and yet it was. The desk was heavy, wooden, and polished in a way that Simon could only describe as "stern." The bookshelves that lined the room were as looming as always. Like dozens of old men staring down at him in disapproval. Maybe because Simon knew the kinds of books that were on those shelves— and what the people who wrote them would think of him and the gaping hole in his chest.

He had money; his family had power. He should be happy, right? Respect his father, respect tradition, tuck his head down and do his best to be a good boy. Be a good *son*.

But he couldn't. He didn't care enough to fight his dad directly like all of his brothers, but he didn't *not* care either.

"I'm sure you've heard about the outright disrespect that's been happening here."

Simon blinked, having forgotten his dad was even there for a minute. What was going on with his mind lately?

"Kind of hard not to."

That wasn't an overstatement. Often it felt like the tension of the conflict was written into the very walls of the house. Like his whole family was obsessed with it; their whole worlds dwindled down to the patriarch versus the new generation. That was part of what grated on Simon's nerves. There was so much else out there to worry about, to learn about, but they were all wrapped up so tightly in their fight that they couldn't see anything else.

"Despite how I raised all of you, despite the fact that all of your brothers owe their success and even their relationships to *my* hard work, they've now turned against me. They've become leftist puppets of those..." His dad faltered, which was an interesting thing to see. What had he been about to say? "... *women* that they've been suckered in by."

Oh. That was what he was going to say. Simon had heard his dad make impolite remarks about women and minorities when in the company of his good ol' boy compatriots, but he'd never seen the man catch himself on those sayings, like he knew they were wrong. Was Dad learning, or was he just trying not to tick Simon off?

"They're running our business to the ground. We've lost *millions* on all these so-called innovations. It's spitting on our legacy, and—"

Simon held up his hand which, surprisingly, actually worked to cut his dad off.

"I don't care."

His father blinked at him, for all the world looking like a very cross owl, and Simon wondered if he resembled the same thing when he was surprised.

"What?" his dad finally said.

"I said, I don't care. I'm not interested in this little family soap opera. None of it even matters."

McLintoc Miller had once been a tan man, his skin a shining golden. But as his venture took off and his body aged, he'd gone to a much paler pallor. Well, Simon got to watch in real time as bright red rushed up the older man's white, wrinkled neck then across his entire face.

"You disrespectful—" he sputtered again, as if he was holding back other words.

That was interesting too. Simon had never known his dad to hold back his temper. Either he truly was desperate for some sort of ally or... actually, Simon didn't know what the "or" option could be, and perhaps that was why he was so fascinated.

His father continued, "I have made you everything you are. You think you're above us with your education and travels, but it's *my* money that paid for them. You are nothing without me, and I will cut you right back down to nothing if you can't even be bothered to *care* about everything that's blessed you."

"Are you threatening to cut me off?"

"I'll do more than cut you off. I'll drain that trust dry. I'll empty your bank account and return your new truck—don't think I didn't notice that. I'll have the lawyers draw something up so every investment you've ever made with my seed money will come back to me. Do you think I won't do this, son? Think your diplomas will somehow save you?"

"I don't think you really want to go there dad," Simon said coolly.

The red on his father's face deepened to almost purple. "You think I won't?"

"You know how upset mom would get if you did that to me. She'd probably never forgive you."

There was a very pregnant pause as his dad digested what he said. Simon guessed that he hadn't even thought about that at all, which meant none of his brothers had used that angle. That was especially surprising considering what a mama's boy Sal was.

"You say that like I'm afraid of my own wife." Dad's voice was low, dangerous.

But Simon let it roll right over him. Because, in the end, he knew exactly how the conversation was going to end.

"Afraid? No, not at all. But I do think you're afraid of losing the last person in this family who actually wants to be around you, and there's nothing more terrifying than being alone and buried in all this gold you've built up around yourself."

Silence. Complete and utter silence. His dad stared at him, opened his mouth, closed it again, then swallowed. He looked a mix between thoroughly shocked and trying to come up with some sort of response.

But there really didn't need to be one, so Simon tipped his head. "We'll talk later, Dad. I've got some research to do."

McLintoc didn't try to stop him as he exited, closing the door politely behind him. But as Simon strode down the hall to his smaller wing, he couldn't help but wonder if maybe his dad felt that same emptiness as him, but instead of trying to find a purpose, he just kept filling the gap with money.

Money was nice, sure, but Simon knew from experience it only took the edge off of the void. No matter how many dollar bills went into it, the hole was always there.

$$5$$

Leilani

She never would have thought it before, but ranch life suited Leilani.

There were so many positives about it, all stacking on top of her to make her feel more at home than she ever had since she'd moved to the mainland. Occasionally, when the blisters on her hands were especially stinging, or when her back was radiating fire from hard work all day, she liked to mentally go through all of them so she could feel that lovely glow of contentment beginning to build inside of her.

She loved being in the sun, first of all. She'd lost some of her color since she left her sunny island where she swam and gardened most of the day, and then worked the dinner and closing shifts at a local restaurant. But now some of it was coming back, warm and rich and wonderful.

She loved being with the animals. They had such personalities! There was Peggy, who absolutely was the queen of the pigpen. There was also Atticus, a mischievous goat who had decided that Leilani's braid was his favorite thing to pull. She'd taken to carrying an extra elastic tie in her pocket to twist her braid into a bun whenever she was in the goats' area.

And of course, there were the cats. Some of them were terrified and hissy—mostly the ones caught in the humane traps—but most ranged from tolerating her presence to outright demanding affection. There was Lady Tamara, a tortie with a truly magnificent tail. Oxford, an orange and white one with a tail that was permanently curved like a comma. Coco, a completely white cat that Frenchie named because she thought that was hilarious, and snowflake, a completely black cat except for one little white splotch in the middle of his forehead. Yeah, Frenchie named that one too.

Leilani had been surprised when she'd first met the tiny woman. When she heard that she was the fiancée of Solomon, the supposed heir to the next generation of the Texas Millers, she had expected someone posh, blond, and more than a little condescending. Frenchie was anything but. She was a svelte lady who bubbled over with creative energy that reminded Leilani a lot of her mother. And, although the girl was almost always smiling, Leilani could see a sort of hardness in her eyes.

Frenchie had obviously seen some things. And for some reason, that made Leilani feel that much more comfortable around her.

Thankfully, she got along well with most of the workers too, and Elizabeth was around just enough for Leilani to never feel lost or uncertain. It was amazing not to be micromanaged by numbers or hounded for productivity, and Leilani didn't realize how stressed she'd been from the constant demands for perfection from her other jobs. And it helped that Nova was a fun one since the Brit-but-not-a-Brit was whom Leilani interacted with the most, even if the tall woman did sometimes get down on herself.

It was safe to say, after a full month of working with the Millers, that she was edging toward finally being comfortable.

And wasn't that something?

One month and suddenly she wasn't worried about rent. She didn't have to not-eat until she could get her free meal at the diner. She didn't have to scrimp and save and still eat nothing but rice for a week outside of work. She *loved* rice, she was an islander after all, but seven days of only a bowl or two while working a pair of jobs had her longing for *something* else.

Her phone bill was paid instead of being constantly a month behind. And she was *saving*. It was incredible. She didn't like to think too far ahead because it was always so easy to jinx things, but imagining what it might be like having the job for six months... a year? It was incredible.

Granted, being outside as the early summer shifted into the *true* summer was very, very *sweaty*.

It wasn't like the islands, which obviously was a warm place. There wasn't a fresh breeze off the ocean, making it much more stifling. In the city it was even worse, with the sunlight and heat refracting off of all the steel and glass.

So naturally, when she was out releasing a cat on a ninety-eight-degree day, she paused when she spotted a big ol' manmade pond complete with a dock.

Oh boy, did that look *nice*.

Leilani couldn't even remember the last time that she had gone swimming. It seemed like forever ago, maybe even before she left the islands. She'd been so busy running, working, and surviving that she had forgotten one of her favorite hobbies.

Could she swim there? Probably not. There had to be a

reason she never heard about it or saw anyone use it… right? Or what if it was a rich people thing to just have a pond and never use it? Leilani was still getting used to some of the ways the Millers worked, and perhaps that was just another example of what happened when one family made just *way* too much money.

"I guess I'll just have to ask."

Nodding to herself, Leilani finished up releasing the cat. He was a shyer one, and he clung to the back of the carrier for a solid ten minutes. But Leilani was a grown human and he was a nervous animal, so she merely backed several feet away and sat down.

It was something that was actually pretty beautiful to watch. How he slowly inched forward, his nose sniffing at the outdoors, uncertain of everything. But little by little, he crept, until his front half was out of the carrier, his head tilted toward the sky with his beautiful pumpkin eyes.

Then his second half came out and he stood there a moment, frozen, before racing off into the field. Another one headed off to live his wild life.

Leilani felt a surge of satisfaction as she stood and packed up the crate. It was so much different working with living creatures. She felt more fulfilled than she ever had by getting a big tip or receiving a glowing customer compliment. Here on the ranch, she was making a difference for all sorts of animals who would possibly not be getting the attention they deserved, and that was a *good* feeling.

Such a good feeling, she almost would have skipped back to her golf cart. Except skipping with her figure lead to a whole lot of jiggling and jostling of things that didn't need to be jiggled or jostled in her work uniform, so she just settled for grinning the entire way back.

She didn't have her own golf cart, like each of the brothers, Elizabeth, Frenchie, and Mrs. Miller did, but she did share one with Nova and another borderline mysterious woman named Teddy.

Teddy was a redhead and about as pale as one could get, with an equally white shock of hair by one of her temples. Leilani didn't know if the woman dyed it that way purposefully or if she just had some sort of skin condition like vitiligo, but she hadn't gotten to know the woman well enough to ask.

She wanted to, however. First of all, her name was Teddy, which was a cute nickname. Secondly, she seemed to be pretty funny from the short experience Leilani had with her. But *thirdly*, her figure was incredibly similar to Leilani's, but with bigger muscles on her arms and slightly thinner thighs. Now that normally wasn't a very important thing, but the one time Leilani had met her at length, the woman was in a well-fitted retro outfit complete with wedges and old-fashioned stockings. Leilani absolutely wanted to pepper her with questions about where the woman shopped.

After all, the young woman finally had money to treat herself, so surely buying a dress wasn't the worst investment. Even if she still felt a *little* guilty in the back of her mind about dropping money on something as short-term as fashion.

"You look like you're deep in thought."

"Huh!?" Leilani nearly launched herself through the plastic roof of the golf cart, not realizing that she'd been idling in front of the place she was supposed to park it for at least a few minutes.

"Whoa, sorry to startle you there. You alright?"

Leilani placed a hand over her thundering heart and looked over her shoulder to see Silas standing there, a bemused expression on his face. He was just about as handsome as all of the Miller boys, but he also had the kindest eyes in her opinion. Even his twin, Sterling, didn't have quite the same vulnerability there.

Or maybe she was just biased because he was the one who had set up all the paperwork for her pay.

But apparently Silas was engaged to the mysterious Teddy —and had done a whole public proposal after a big community event in the city—which only made her want to know more about the both of them.

"I'm fine," she said with a laugh. "Just startled me, is all."

"You know, my brothers have been complaining about me and Sterling doin' that to 'em all the time. Say we walk too quiet, or something. I just think y'all have a habit of getting into your own heads."

"Maybe that's it." She shut off the golf cart then crossed to the key rack to hang up her set. It wasn't until she was turning back around that she remembered the question she was supposed to ask. "Hey, Silas, what's with the pond out to the west of the house?"

"What do you mean?"

"Why haven't I seen anyone use it?"

"Oh, no reason. Mostly we're just so busy. It's not toxic or anything. We made sure it had a good enough ecosystem in there to be a swimming hole and not breed mosquito larvae or anything like that. I *hate* those skeeters."

"I'm not exactly a fan of them either."

"I imagine most people aren't. But why do you ask?"

"I just wanted to know. It looks so nice there, and this is swimming season if there ever was one." She let out a gentle sigh, thinking of the clear waters of Waikiki or snorkeling at Hanauma Bay. Sure, the latter was pretty tourist-heavy, but when she had friends or cousins visit from the mainland, it was a great way to give them a crash course in the beauty and bounty of the ocean. "It's the kind of place it'd be nice to have a birthday party. You know, like some shade, a blanket to lay on, and snacks with a few friends."

She could almost see it in her head. She hadn't had a party since she left the islands. They always reminded her too much of everything she missed. But something about that pond seemed... set apart.

"Oh, why don't you then?"

Leilani paused in her daydream, trying to reel herself back to the present. "Why don't I what?"

"Do that. Throw a birthday party. Unless your birthday isn't actually in the summer and you were just waxing poetically."

"Uh, no, actually. To the waxing. I mean, the poetical stuff." Ah, she was getting flustered. But how could she not be when her employer was offering her something so offhandedly. Something *important.* "I mean, my birthday is coming up in two weeks, and I would absolutely love to have a party at the pond, if you are alright with me inviting a couple of people."

"Sounds fine by me. Just email me the date and all that so I can get you the day off work."

"Day off... I was just going to hold it on the weekend."

He shrugged. "If that's more convenient for you, then okay. But I've always been partial to celebrating it the day of."

"Right. Day of. Of course." Wow, the Millers really were something else. "Well then, it's on the fourteenth. And uh, I would love it if all of you came."

"All of us?"

Something about his question made her feel like she had misspoken. "Yeah, you, your mom, your brothers and all their girls. I'm going to text Nova and Elizabeth directly, but I don't have Frenchie or Teddy's numbers?"

"Really? That's surprising. I know Teddy's been wanting to get her hands on your car."

Wait, what? "She has?"

"Yeah, it's basically a right of passage, getting your car worked on by Teddy when you get hired here. She used to work here too, but now we just contract that out. Makes it easier with me not being directly her boss."

"Only indirectly?"

He let out a laugh at that. "No one on earth could ever indirectly boss Teddy about anything, and that's a fact."

Wow. Leilani definitely needed to get to know this woman. "Well I look forward to her coming to my party."

He tipped his head. "I'll send the invitation out for you. Just send me an email with the time you'd like us all to be there, and we can have a right nice get together. You know you don't have to invite us, right?"

"I know less than a handful of people on the mainland. I'd love to have y'all there. Besides, it'd be awkward to just invite Nova and Elizabeth but nobody else who I see here all the time."

"The mainland?"

"Yeah, you know, the continental United States."

"Oh." He seemed to think for a minute. "As opposed to..."

"Alaska, Hawaii or any of the multiple territories, like Puerto Rico and America Samoa in the South Pacific."

"Right, you're *Hawaiian*. That explains the name."

Leilani leveled him with a look. "You literally did my online boarding paperwork with me and entered it into the system."

"Yes, you're right. But you marked Caucasian and other for ethnicities, so I never thought to ask further."

Oh right, she had done that. It was something that became a habit when she moved to the mainland and Leilani's resume kept getting rejected, while using the name Lani Cunningham got her more interviews. Of course, there was always the slight bump of when the interviewer was surprised that a brown person showed up, but whatever. Leilani had managed to land a waitressing job that at least got her to above water—even if she was always *this* close to drowning.

"That's what you get for not being nosey, I guess."

"Hah, it seems so. You have a good day now, Miss Leilani."

"Thanks, Silas."

He tipped his head to her then continued into his own cart. If she had to guess where he was going, she would put money on it that it was to see his horse. The story Leilani had heard was that the poor girl had had a *very* bad fall a while back, and while she was almost completely recovered, he still babied her a lot. Which, of course, all the women of the ranch seemed to think was pretty adorable. Who didn't like a handsome man with a soft spot for those he cared about?

Leilani's smile quickly fled from her face. She didn't need to be thinking about any men at all. Sure, plenty of them seemed kind, but plenty weren't actually, and the only way to find out was to get to know them.

Which was acutely dangerous.

Shaking her head, she shoved all that away. She had a birthday party to plan! She was going to invite Cindy and Lou from the diner, and Auntie Kini so it wouldn't just be a Miller-fest, but she couldn't wait.

And that same anticipation bubbled within her all the way until her shift was over. Almost as soon as she was in the car, she placed her phone in its holder so she could video chat her mother for the long drive home.

Of course, her mom picked up on only the second ring, her tired face coming into focus on the screen.

"Ah, there's my beautiful girl. How are you? It's been a few days."

"*Ma'i ka'i,*" Leilani responded out of habit before remembering that she actually had good news. "My employers gave me permission to have a birthday party at their swimming hole! Even gave me the day off."

"Oh really? These are those new employers, right? The one with the handsome man who offered you a job out of nowhere?"

"I didn't say he was handsome, Mom."

"What, you think I was born too long ago to use the internet? I looked this Miller family up." She waved her hand in front of her face. "I know they're all *haoles*, but that family's bone structure is amazing."

"*Mom.*"

"What, you think your mom doesn't have eyes? I'm always looking out for a cute boy for my girl."

"Are you purposefully trying to embarrass me, or are you just feeling extra mom-ish today."

"Probably both. I always like to be versatile, you know."

That got a laugh out of both of them. Leilani knew many people who did not have good relationships with their parents; she knew people who were hurt, hit, or just mercilessly made to feel awful. She would be forever grateful that she and her mother had a wonderful bond. Even though she was twenty-two, about to be twenty-three, she would be lost without Mom.

And she'd also do anything to protect her.

That's why she was on the mainland in the first place, and why she stayed on the mainland even when her mother wistfully sighed about missing her and wishing she was back home. All the alienation, all the homesickness was worth it if her family was safe.

"I'm proud of you. You know that, right?"

Leilani nodded. "Thanks, Mom. I don't mind hearing it every once and a while, even if you've already told me. Any..." She hesitated a moment, looking in the background of the video call for her younger siblings. She couldn't be sure who was around, so she just decided to go with something neutral. "...news?"

Naturally her mother didn't need any more explanation. "No. I'm sorry, my love. Nothing."

"Nothing is better than something bad, I suppose," Leilani said, steeling herself from the sigh that wanted to escape her lips.

"That it is. We'll get through this. All of us."

That was where that particular conversation ended, and they drifted to other things. Her little sister Malia was suddenly very into painting and nail polish, so naturally everyone in the house had their fingers and toes done up in fun colors. Maybe some would be surprised that Leilani's brothers would let their littlest sister doll them up, but it was no secret that Malia had all of them wrapped around her chubby fingers. Even at the age of nine, she was the baby of their house and her brothers had already dedicated themselves as her bodyguards.

Leilani couldn't help but wonder if they were that way because of everything that had happened with *her*. They had been too young, and she was the eldest, after all. She wasn't supposed to need *them* to protect her. But she still felt like sometimes she could see the guilt on their features, their wishes that they had done something to...

But that was ridiculous. They were kids, and so was she, and sometimes life was just cruel. The important thing was to pick up and keep moving.

And so she did. The conversation flowed from topic to

topic, with plenty of laughter. Before Leilani knew it, she was in the city and had to end the call. Hands-free talking and driving was one thing while on a flat stretch of road, but it was another entirely when she was doing city driving.

By the time she made it home, she was rightly exhausted, but called her family back while she was making dinner. It was still early for them, but her mom's night job made it easy for their schedules to sync up for frequent video chats.

Which Leilani was eternally grateful for. Sure, she was separated physically from her family, but that didn't mean she couldn't be with them spiritually. Couldn't talk to them and make sure that they were safe. Share in the wonderful parts of everyday life that she was so afraid of missing.

Her dinner was more involved than usual, if only because she could now afford fresh ingredients. As she went about making some grilled talapia, her mother handed her off to Malia, who talked all about color theory—which was an interesting thing to hear a nine-year-old describe.

By the time her meal and the call ended, and she went through her nightly routine, Leilani was more than ready for bed. She practically threw herself on her futon and—for just a few moments—allowed herself to have faith that life was going to keep on getting better.

She'd finally turned the corner and, for once, there weren't any ghosts behind it.

6

Leilani

*I*t was her birthday!

Leilani's leg was practically bouncing as she drove herself to the Miller's place about two hours before her festivities were supposed to start. She knew it was unorthodox, but she was still completely jazzed that they were letting her throw a shindig on their property.

It wasn't like she was some long-time employee that they had all these bonds with. She had only been there a month and a half and, as far as they knew, she could be the world's worst person.

And yet, there she was, driving along the rarely used dirt path that led to the pond.

Someone had obviously gotten there before her—because there were little pickets with signs attached to them, arrows drawn with a bright red marker with hibiscus drawn in the corners. Leilani knew Frenchie had to be behind that, and she was incredibly flattered that the girl remembered how important those flowers were to many Hawaiians.

And they were definitely important to Leilani. It was even in her name: heavenly flower. Her mother said she'd named her that because it was the only thing on the earth that seemed to be ever close to as beautiful as her new baby. Of course, that always got Leilani to blushing and quickly changing the subject.

It wasn't that she thought she was ugly. Leilani was well aware that she was attractive to a good number of people, as much as anyone could expect to be considering that one couldn't please everyone. She was also well aware that some people got *very* angry that they were attracted to her, or that some people were angry that *other* people were attracted to her, and that almost always had to do with the fact that she was fat.

Some people hated that word, but it was just another descriptor to Leilani. She was tall, fat and pretty. None of them were mutually exclusive. In fact, her generous figure was one of the things she loved the most about herself. She loved the wide curve of her hip, how her waist nipped in. She loved her softness just as much as she loved her strength.

No, Leilani didn't mind all of the bumps that came along with being a plus-sized woman in a skinny-obsessed world. What she minded was what always seemed to happen when the wrong person was attracted to her. Because there was always someone. Whether it was a grabby patron, or a flirty coworker or—

No. She wasn't going to think about that. Not on her birthday.

Donning her crown once again as the Queen of Compartmentalization, Leilani parked her car in the adorable little roped-off lot and headed toward the pond.

She was speechless before she even got there, however, as she could see that the Millers had already gotten there before her and set up. And they hadn't just laid out some tables and chairs. They'd erected a whole *tent* for her! One of those fancy ones they used at festivals that was the prettiest shade of robin's egg blue. There were chairs, a grill, and she even spotted one of those giant floaties in the pond!

"Do you like it?" Frenchie called, bounding over to her with a wide grin. "I tried to order you some hibiscus, but apparently they wouldn't come in time. But just like, imagine they're all around the tent, okay?"

"This is amazing," Leilani breathed, feeling tears prick at the corners of her eyes. Was she dreaming? People on the mainland didn't just throw lavish birthday parties for each other... did they? Was this the southern hospitality that she had heard so much about? "I can't believe you did all this."

"Honestly, this isn't even that much. I went through years of my life never being able to celebrate a birthday party, so now I tend to go overboard. Besides, Nova talks about you a lot, so I figured this would be just as fun for them as it is you!"

"She does?"

"Yeah! You've made it so much easier on her. She's been wanting to cut back her hours so she can study more and take online classes."

That made Leilani's chest warm. She liked Nova, but she had never been quite sure if it was reciprocated. Nova just seemed friendly with everyone.

"Anyway, let me show you what all we cooked!"

"You cooked?"

Frenchie took her hand, lacing their fingers together as she guided them to the tent. Sure enough, there were finger foods, little tea snacks, some delicious looking cookies, then both a veggie and a fruit tray that looked hand made more than store-bought.

"You really shouldn't have," Leilani said, her chest getting tight. She didn't know these people, didn't know them at all, and yet they'd done all this for her birthday.

"We're glad you like it. I'll admit, we were all ready to rein Francesca in, but Simon said we should let her throw you a real shindig. I hope we didn't overstep," Mrs. Miller said.

"Simon?" Leilani repeated. That was the youngest, right? The one who hired her?

"Yeah. He'll deny it, of course, but he was adamant that we treat it like any of our own birthdays. Not that we wouldn't, but some people absolutely hate surprises, you know?"

Oh, Leilani knew. She had a cousin like that. But she hadn't seen the Simon guy since she was hired, and she thought he'd just disappeared for a while. Like he was the business traveling brother or something.

"Is he here?"

"He's hauling ice from the house with Sal. Should be rollin' right up any moment. Now, did you bring anything that we need to put into the coolers?"

"What? Oh! Yeah, I did."

Leilani tried to get her brain back on track, but she was so high on the warm and fuzzies that it was harder than it should have been. Maybe it was silly to be so flattered by a tent and some food, but it *meant* something to her. That she was seen and noticed and that the folks around her cared enough to throw her a party just to celebrate being born.

Amazing.

"Let me run to the car and get it!"

She wasn't even embarrassed about the meager supplies she had brought. She'd spent more than she ever had on her own birthday, but it still paled in comparison to the spread that the Millers had laid out.

Nevertheless, she grabbed her bags of chips, cheap soda, pretzels, and cheese tray then headed to the tent. She was still arranging stuff and putting things into coolers when Simon returned with the ice and his other brother, Sal. Leilani had seen the truly large Miller a couple of times just as a side effect from getting to know Nova, but *man*, did she forget how huge he was every single time. What did Mrs. Miller *feed* that boy?

Not that she should call him a boy. He was older than her. She was pretty sure she was the youngest of the group, or at least that she and Nova were tied. Funny, how no one ever infantilized her despite that.

But it wasn't the hulking son her eyes stayed on, but rather Simon, the youngest. The one who had given her that big chance. The one who changed her life.

He had the same stunning looks as most of his brothers, but he was also different. Mostly in the eyes. And it was only after a few more minutes of staring that she realized he had almost the exact same ones his father had. She wouldn't have known if she hadn't researched them so thoroughly before she took the job —as she had never met the patriarch—but once she connected those two ideas in her head, it was impossible not to see it.

He was well built, like his brothers, but while his shoulders were broader, his waist was narrower, almost like an upside-down triangle or Dorito chip. It reminded her of Olympian swimmers or how superheroes tended to look recently in the movies. Minus the biceps the size of her head. Sal had that on lock.

He didn't look like the youngest, but she supposed once

everyone was near their mid-twenties, it got harder to say. He did look *young,* however. Not so old that it was creepy he had asked her out.

"Simon?" she asked tentatively, crossing over to him. He was a strange sort of enigma to her. He'd asked her out, took her refusal well, offered her a job, then promptly ignored or avoided her. She couldn't tell if he was playing some sort of long con or if he was a genuine person who felt guilty for putting her on the spot. The latter one seemed almost impossible, however. Especially from a complete stranger.

The man stopped dead still, a big bag of ice in his hands that he was clearly transferring from the wheelbarrows he and his brother had brought over to one of the coolers. "Yes?"

Why did he look so terrified? Like she'd stabbed him or something.

"I just wanted to say thank you."

He wavered at that, and she felt like she could see something underneath his charming, confident exterior. Something uncertain and just a little vulnerable.

"I didn't—"

"Your mom told me that you were the one who convinced them to set Frenchie loose. I couldn't have anticipated this at all. Thank you, really, for making this an amazing day."

"The party hasn't even started yet."

Goodness, the man had a hard time taking a compliment. But his mother had said that he would try to deny it. That was fine with Leilani. She understood being humble even if she didn't understand how she'd found such wonderful people. For the first time in literal years, she felt a sort of welcome, peace and safety she hadn't in ages.

She was so caught up in the emotions, in her gratitude, that she didn't think. She just swept forward and caught him up in a hug, squeezing him tight enough that she hoped he could *feel* her happiness radiating off of her.

"You have no idea how much I appreciate this," she said before untangling herself and stepping back. She meant to say more, heck she felt like she could give a whole speech, but then Frenchie was grabbing her hand again and hauling her toward the punch, talking the whole while. She'd read about this passion fruit-orange-guava drink, called POG, during her planning but wanted Leilani to show her how to make it how she herself liked it.

Of course, Leilani didn't have an objection to that. Like any Polynesian raised on the islands, she sure did love POG. And it was something she rarely made for herself because of all the sugar.

She was barely done mixing it by the time Cindy pulled up with Auntie Kini in the car next to her. Before the older woman was even out, Leilani bounded over to both of them, enveloping them in a fierce hug one right after the other.

"Wow, this is quite the set up you have here," her auntie said, letting out a low whistle as she took Leilani's arm. "You do this all yourself?"

"I couldn't even dream of it. Nah, the Millers set this up. Can you—"

"Auntie Kini, is that you?"

Leilani looked up sharply as someone called her Auntie that wasn't her. The next thing she knew, Nova was bounding over with open arms.

"Nova! I didn't know you knew my Leilani."

"Hold on," Leilani said, trying to catch up. "How do *you* know each other?"

"We go to the same physical therapy office," Nova said, releasing the other woman from her hug and stepping back.

"Oh my gosh, I can't believe that you're one of her eleventy-billion nieces and nephews."

"Twenty-seven," Auntie Kini said before there was a shout from by the tent.

"Auntie!"

And then Frenchie was running over, her arms open too. "Auntie!"

Leilani watched with wide eyes as the older woman hugged Frenchie too, the two of them actually fairly close in height. "Wait, how do *you* two know each other now?"

"I met Auntie Kini in a church I like to visit now and again when I need to clear my mind. She gave me valuable advice."

"I just like to listen," Auntie said, her wrinkled hands gently cupping Frenchie's face. "And look how you've flourished, my child. I couldn't be more proud."

Frenchie flushed from head to toe, and something clicked in Leilani's brain.

"Wait, is Frenchie the girl you told me about who is helping run the homeless connection program through your church?"

"Oh, you've heard about my program?" the smaller woman asked with a wide grin. "Auntie Kini, you *do* talk about me."

"Of course, I do. I talk about all my babies."

Leilani's mind was reeling. Forget six degrees of separation. Apparently two of the people at the Miller's ranch were already close with someone in her family and she'd had no idea. What were the chances?

"But you haven't been at Bible study in ages, Francesca. Have you become too busy for an old woman?" Leilani instantly recognized the go-to guilt trip that her Auntie loved to use and cleared her throat.

"Come see the spread they made. You're going to be real impressed," Leilani said.

"I'm already impressed. It's so funny how we really do make *ohana* wherever we go, isn't that right?"

Frenchie and Nova both nodded emphatically. Leilani was still trying to compute how on earth it happened that they were already so interconnected, and none of them knew, when there was the sound of a car pulling up behind them.

"Sorry I'm late," came the lower, somewhat raspy voice that Leilani instantly recognized as Teddy.

Craning her neck, she saw the curvy mechanic step out of her vehicle, a large basket of what looked like fresh flowers and vegetables of different colors. "I ended up finding more harvestable things than I thought I would." She grinned brightly, her burgundy painted lips parting to reveal white teeth. She was wearing another retro outfit, a pink gingham crop top with bell sleeves and black, high waisted bell bottoms.

Leilani *really* needed to find out where the woman shopped.

"I hope you like these," Teddy continued, striding forward in that confident way of hers that made Leilani pretty sure the woman could be an adept surfer. "I heard that you're a fan of most everything but eggplant?"

"As far as I know," Leilani said, turning the rest of the way to introduce her company. "Everyone, this is my friend Cindy—sorry for ignoring you there for a moment."

"Oh, I don't mind," the waitress drawled. "It was right amusin' to see the looks on y'all faces for that whole shenanigan."

"Shenanigans? Y'all getting into things without—" The mechanic stopped dead in her tracks. "*You.*"

"Me," Auntie Kini said with a laugh. "Goodness, what a day. How did your situation end up turning out? I never did end up seeing you again. I've visited the gardens a couple of times, hoping maybe I could catch an update."

It had to be a prank. It *had* to. And yet the recognition in the redhead's eyes seemed entirely genuine.

"I've only been once or twice since. But I can't believe this. You know Leilani?"

"Leilani is the daughter of my favorite niece," Auntie Kini said with a smile. "I babysat her for a short while before I moved to the mainland."

"And gave me a place to stay when I moved here," Leilani added. She knew the older woman always liked to downplay the good that she did for everyone, something that was very firmly being reiterated considering the situation that was unfolding right in front of them. "You guys met at the botanical gardens?"

Teddy nodded. "I was struggling with making some choices and whether to open myself up to the scary possibility of someone who I considered out of my league loving me." She held up her hand where the demure ring she wore glittered. "You can infer that she gave me some good advice."

"Oh! Look at that! Let me see it up close!" Auntie Kini let go of Leilani's arm and strode forward, her limp from her hip nonexistent.

Although Leilani was still incredulous at the situation, she was happy to see her relative so happy.

The older woman took Teddy's hand and oohed and aahed over it, the two seeming to have a grand old time. Meanwhile, Nova and Frenchie were exchanging surprised looks and talking about how they knew Auntie Kini and the probability of it all.

"I gotta say," Cindy said, stepping up to Leilani and

throwing an arm over her shoulder. "For being from a tiny island, your tata there sure does know how to make friends."

"Tata? That another southern phrase I don't know?" Leilani countered with a laugh. Of all of her acquaintances, Cindy had the thickest accent of anyone she knew. The younger woman said she lived in Alabama until she was fifteen and lived with her Cajun aunt and uncle, who basically adopted her.

"It means Auntie, silly. Don't get me started on all the slang you use, Ms. *Uku* and *Poke*."

"Alright, fair enough."

There was the sound of two more cars pulling in, and then Lou, her former coworker, was stepping out, then Elizabeth from her vehicle. Leilani held her breath, wondering if the vet somehow knew her Auntie, but the dark-skinned woman just smiled warmly.

"Hello, and here I thought I was early. Did I miss the introductions?"

"No," Leilani said before a laugh rumbled through her. "You might be the only person who needs one."

That cracked up Nova as well, leaving Lou and Elizabeth to look uncertainly at all the laughter. Leilani would explain it, she would, but it was all just so *funny*.

It was going to be a great birthday, she knew it.

Leilani drove her auntie home with a full belly and thoroughly exhausted in the best way possible. Her arms hurt, her legs hurt, and her skin was warm from the sun in a way that let her know that she was going to tan.

She'd even gotten to swim for a couple hours, her and Nova splashing around with Sal and Silas while Frenchie carefully waded with both Solomon and Teddy teaching her how to doggy paddle. Elizabeth sat on the dock with Sterling, both of them looking sappy and in love while they dangled their feet in the water. The only ones who didn't really join were the older folks and Simon, who sat in the tent and watched contentedly. Even Cindy and Lou took off their shoes and walked around the very edge of the pond, hand in hand.

Now that part Leilani had been *very* interested to see. She had thought that the two would be cute together—they had excellent chemistry—but as far as she knew they were still playing the will-they-won't-they game. She knew it was tricky dating coworkers, but she was glad to see that maybe the two of them were working something out.

It also made her heart ache. A sort of longing that she wasn't used to. She'd always told herself she didn't need romance, that having anyone be interested in her wasn't worth the hassle. After all, with what had happened—

Nope.

It was her birthday and she had a wonderful day. She wasn't going to let *him* invade her thoughts and bring her down. She was moving on and forward. And if she kept saving up money, in a year or two she might be able to go home and not worry about things.

She looked to Auntie Kini, who was dozing while leaned back in her seat. The older woman had seemed to thoroughly enjoy herself and even made a friend in Mrs. Miller. It still completely blew Leilani's mind that Nova, Frenchie, and Teddy all knew her favorite and closest auntie, but in a way, it made sense. Before Leilani had moved to the mainland, her mom had always worried about their relative, saying that she seemed lonely. After all, she'd moved to the States to take care of her own *hapa* daughter, only for her to pass away from cancer.

Then her husband had divorced her to run off with someone about half her age, leaving the older woman all alone. Leilani had always wondered why Auntie Kini hadn't just moved back to the islands, but she'd insisted that she'd found a place in her community and fallen in love with Dallas.

Finally, Leilani got it. At least a little bit. If the city was full of people like the Millers and their partners, full of Cindys and Lous, maybe she could carve herself out a home too.

...she just wished it was more her choice and less what was forced on her.

Ugh, that wasn't a good way to think. She was doing the best she could, and she was surrounded by wonderful people. And she'd just had one of the most magical days in years. It was even immortalized on the internet, Nova taking a selfie of all of them together before posting it to her profile and tagging Leilani so they could follow each other. They were going to share *so* many animal and ranch photos, she knew it.

Yeah, some awful things had gotten her on her path, but at least she was in a wonderful place now.

Smiling, Leilani hummed to herself as she played the perfect day over in her head. She couldn't imagine a single thing that would make it better except if she was somehow back home.

What a great day.

7

———

Simon

Simon was having such a bad day.

He couldn't imagine a single thing that could make it worse, except maybe another family function like his graduation dinner.

Granted, it *had* been fun to watch his dad turn purple, but ultimately not worth the high drama that came after it. As far as he knew, his cousins out to the west hadn't contacted their side of the family since. Which was a shame. He liked his cousins there, the only girl Millers in their generation and one lone son. Especially since the eldest one had been so ready to go to bat for him.

But anyway, cousins or no, he was not having a good time. He was looking into new master's programs, trying to find something to feed his starving brain. He'd been home a total of two months and was already going *crazy*.

There were just enough changes on the ranch that nothing felt familiar. But there was also just enough the same that so much of it seemed mired and never changing. He was caught between contempt for his family, whose worlds held so little, while not having a world of his own at all.

There had been a couple of bright spots. Making breakfast with his mom. Playing ball with Sal. And Leilani's birthday.

That had been a very good day.

Seeing her smile, seeing her laugh, she was like a literal ray of light in all the haze that he always seemed surrounded by. It gave him a deep sense of satisfaction to see her having the time of her life. There was that sense of purpose he had been looking for.

But then the day ended and that was over.

Of course, he hadn't forgotten how it felt when she'd hugged him, her body warm and incredibly soft against him. He'd wanted to wrap his arms around her and hold on to that feeling she gave him, the one where the floor was solid and not everything seemed too empty, but before he knew it Frenchie was whisking her away.

He wished he could hold her again, long enough to parse out every single detail of what it felt like to have her in his arms, but he couldn't. He was her boss, she was an employee, and she'd already turned him down. Besides, a woman like her *had* to be taken. There was no way she wasn't. With how kind, personable and hard-working she was, it was easy to see how she had probably been snatched up the moment she'd come to the continental US.

Or maybe it was someone back home? That would make sense why she never seemed to mention having someone around. And while Simon always tried to give her space, he'd seen her video-chatting multiple times on her breaks or after work, sitting in her car and laughing for a while before eventually driving off. Given the time difference between Hawaii and Texas, that certainly made sense.

Simon shook his head, focusing back on the internet page in front of him. He needed to get his mind off Leilani. He didn't want to be a creep, but he kind of *felt* like a creep, pining over an employee he barely talked to.

Or maybe that was just because he'd never really pined for anyone in his life.

Well... except for a particular Warrior Princess that had been on TV when he'd been a kid. That had been a crush of his all the way up until midway through puberty. Something about a warrior cry and a weapon apparently appealed to younger Simon.

But Leilani was the first *real* person he'd ever pined over, and he certainly didn't appreciate the feeling. There were beautiful women who'd been thrilled to date him in every port, and while they'd been lovely for an evening's dinner, or dancing in the moonlight, none of them ever affected him like Leilani did.

And she'd done so with only a smile and some friendly conversation. That was it. She'd hooked him so effortlessly and she didn't even know it.

He needed to get away. From his family, from the ranch, and from seeing Leilani as she made friends wherever she went. But where should a man go who's already been around the world and back?

Camping!

The idea came to him like a bolt of lightning. He used to go camping all the time. First with all of his brothers, then with Boy Scouts, then with just Sal. It had always been fun and a nice escape from the world. Simon had always loved being with nature. Although he'd pretty much felt unsettled and directionless since he was an adult, being out in it took the edge off of those discomforts. Sure, it didn't make him forget, but it was like a… balm. A sort of holdover.

Quickly he texted his mom that he was going to take the weekend to camp. She texted him right back with exactly where all the supplies were. While Simon wasn't as meticulously organized as her, he definitely appreciated her mother-ability of remembering exactly where everything was.

Except her keys. If there was one thing that almost everyone in the family knew, it was that Mom would lose her keys about once a day if she didn't immediately hang them on the rack by the door. That was why they had three copies of the set to her golf cart.

In the end, it took less than three hours for him to load up all the supplies he needed into his truck and take off down the highway. It wasn't a far drive, about an hour, but it was the way to one of the trails that he remembered the strongest in his mind. Back in the day, he and Sal would go to blow off steam before he got into bodybuilding. They'd talk about bullies, about the annoying cliques in school, and how difficult it was coming up in the shadow of their brothers, all who were popular in school.

Not that Simon was ever bothered too much. He had his own group of friends and was generally well-liked, but he was nowhere near as popular as the twins had been. Or even Samuel, who had been the quiet type but so nice that everyone got along with him.

He arrived at the trail just as afternoon was setting in, the sun beating down, and the shade of the trees was certainly a mercy. He drove his truck along the part of the path that was meant for it, before pulling aside at one of the many natural groves that people tended to set up in.

The ritual of making his camp was a soothing one. Setting up his tent, his bedroll, making a fire circle, bear-proofing things even though the chances of him running into an actual bear were pretty slim. The whole thing was over far too soon, and he found himself staring at a cozy little site that was all his.

Simon breathed out a sigh of relief, his chest feeling like it was unconstricting, and he thought about making his dinner from the food he had brought. But something in him wasn't ready to settle yet, so he figured maybe trying to catch his own dinner from the river that he knew cut through the area would be a fine way to spend his late-afternoon going into the early evening.

Back into his truck bed, he grabbed all that he needed and then headed out, his backpack heavy but assuring against his shoulder blades and his arms full.

It was a longer trek than he remembered, but he arrived at the lake without getting lost, although the path was harder to see in the hazy gold of the afternoon. But sure enough, the trees thinned, and he saw the gently flowing water ahead.

It wasn't the biggest river. Maybe about ten feet or so across, but there was plenty of game in it. He knew that from experience. So, with a smile on his face, he set up his chair, his bait, his cooler, and got to baiting his hook.

His body fell into a rhythm, breathing, releasing, letting the hook do what it needed to do, then slowly trawling it back in. He'd used bobbins when he was younger, but as he'd grown, he'd migrated away from that.

It took maybe a half-hour, maybe an hour before he got a solid bite, but then he was sitting up in his chair and reeling it in. It put up quite a fight, but he was patient, reeling it in, letting it swim out, resisting enough to exhaust itself but not get free. After a good struggle, he had it up on the shore and deposited it into his cooler. It was a catfish and he figured he could catch one more and then call it a night. He did like his protein, after all.

He was just settling back when he heard noises, and on the other side of the river, a group of three men about his age appeared at the tree line. He watched them carefully, but they seemed to just be simple backpackers, and they waved when they saw him.

He waved back, and they approached with that weary sort of way that hikers did. Simon didn't like to fight—he wasn't even very good at it—so he hoped that his assessment of the group was correct.

"Hey there, getting many bites?"

He had a pleasant sort of accent, but one that Simon couldn't place. It sounded almost Spanish in some way, but there was a lilt and deepness to it that didn't sit right in his brain. It was similar to how he had had difficulty placing Leilani's accent at first, yet this man didn't really sound like her either. It still seemed like he had so much to learn about the world.

"Haven't been here long, but I've gotten one."

"Ah, nice! Not much for the fish around here, but I do love fried catfish."

"Especially in Panko," the one to the first talker's right said, smiling brightly. "You ever try Panko breadcrumbs?"

"I'm not much of a cook," Simon answered, returning the grin. "But I'll keep that in mind."

"Aw, every man should know how to cook for himself," what seemed to be the leader said, pulling a water bottle from one of the side pockets on his backpack. "How else are you gonna treat your lady when you want to make her feel special?"

"I'll tell ya when I get a lady."

That had the three of them laughing and Simon felt himself grin genuinely. He missed this part of traveling, making friends from anywhere and sharing a sort of commonality.

"That's good, cousin, that's good." The leader drank another swig from his bottle.

Simon took the opportunity to give all three an actual look-over. They were golden-skinned with a reddish tint below it, a flush to their cheeks and a sheen across their brow. They'd definitely been hiking it for a good while, that was for sure.

The one at the center was the tallest, with a thick shock of dark hair pulled back into a ponytail, while one was bald and the other had his hair buzzed short. All were muscular in that sort of lean way that laborers had, and the center one had a scar that went from his ear to about halfway across his cheeks.

None of them were people that Simon would want to get into a fight with, but none of them seemed like they wanted to start a fight. No, they seemed genuinely happy and relieved to see another person.

"By the way, cuz, we're on our way to Dallas to visit an old friend of ours. We were debating stopping around here and setting up for the night or continuing on. You got any advice for us strangers? We don't wanna make bad choices out here, ya know."

Simon looked above to the scant amount of sun that made it through the trees. "Honestly, it'd be smart to stop now. It'll be night before you get there. It's a little over a two-and-a half-hour drive back, so you're looking at several hours of walking."

"Whew, that's quite a ways just to go camping. This like your vacay or something?"

"Nah, I live on a ranch about smack dab in the middle. An hour fifteenish."

"A ranch? So what, you're like a cowboy? Ain't never met a real cowboy before."

"I guess you could say that. Don't much feel like it most of the time." Or ever. Maybe if Simon actually felt like a cowboy, he wouldn't have the strange void that was ever-present in him.

"Really? Didn't know that was a way you could feel."

"I guess it is when you're part of a whole cowboy empire."

"An empire?"

Simon nodded. "Yeah, you probably haven't heard of the Miller Ranch, but there's kind of a whole history of ranching floating above my head."

"Ah, I hear you there, man. My old man and his old man before him have been running their own business and were real mad when I decided to go my own way." The man gave an authoritative nod as if he'd come to some sort of conclusion. "Well, thanks for the advice, man. We're gonna find a place to set up our tent and make a fire before it gets too dark. Good luck with your fish."

"Thanks, good luck on the rest of your walk."

"*Mahalo*, cousin."

"*Mahalo*," Simon returned although he didn't know exactly what that meant. He felt like he'd heard it before in passing but couldn't place it. Portuguese maybe? Tagalog?

Before he had a chance to ask, the three were heading off, following the river no doubt to one of the more frequently used groves that might even have a camping grill in it. Simon decided it wasn't worth it for him to delay them and resolved to look it up himself later.

He got several more bites but not another catch before it grew too dark to linger. Packing up, Simon headed back to his camp to clean his fish and start a fire.

And as the stars dotted the sky, he felt the tiniest bit of peace that he'd missed so desperately.

8

Leilani

*L*eilani's life was going so smoothly that it practically felt like a dream. Most days she woke up well-rested and without much worry about how she was going to pay her bills. She had nicer shoes with insoles so that her feet didn't blister and ache every day. She could finally afford to go to her doctor, so she'd gotten checked up and didn't have to worry about an injury making her homeless or a burden on Auntie Kini.

Her car had been looked at by Teddy, who'd done most of the repairs for free, and Leilani had to get *real* insistent to get the redhead to take her money. And in the meantime, she'd finally had the chance to ask the mechanic where she bought her clothes. As it turned out, since Teddy had extra money after dating Silas, she'd made friends with a seamstress down in the southern tier of the city who made all the outfits custom for her. She'd offered to connect the two of them on her next order and Leilani had hastily agreed.

Her lease was up on her studio in about three months, but she wasn't worried about them hiking the rent because she was upgrading to a one-bedroom on the edge of the city, almost in the suburbs, closer to the ranch. Her pants didn't have holes in the thighs and her fridge was stocked with a healthy balance of protein, fresh fruits and veggies, and delicious carbs.

She had time to visit her auntie; she had time to visit her friends. And she was closer than ever with the women of the Miller clan, feeling more and more included with every passing day.

It was wonderful, and even her phone was new and shiny, her new pay finally allowing her to buy an upgrade and case to keep it protected from heavy ranching life. And she owed it all to the youngest Miller.

It was too bad that he still avoided her like the plague. Maybe he had taken offense to her turning him down. She had no idea.

But she didn't let it bother her and went to work every day happy to be there and went home happy to be where she was. Sure, she still missed home, she missed her family. But the stability was *nice* and something she hadn't had when she was nineteen.

"Aw, come on, I made that jump!" she complained to her phone, the character she was playing losing a life as he fell into a pit with rainbow snakes.

"Did I come at a bad time?"

Leilani twisted to look behind where she'd sprawled out across some hay bales on her break. Frenchie was standing there on the ground, a bemused expression on her face.

"Nah, nothing world-ending. Just fat thumbs." Leilani sat up and shaded her eyes. "What's up? Ya need something?"

"No, but you have visitors at the main house."

Visitors? That didn't... "Oh, did Auntie Kini drop by?"

"No." Frenchie's expression grew more serious. "It's a group of young men, said they were your cousins. I love that you feel comfortable here, but Mrs. Miller isn't so hot on strangers she hasn't invited walking up to the front door without being warned."

Men? *Cousins*? Leilani's blood instantly ran cold, her heart squeezing in her chest so hard that she could barely whisper to Frenchie.

"What do they look like?"

"I dunno. Like dudes. I mean, they obviously share your family's good genes because they're pretty handsome. Tanned. One has long hair, one's bald and one was, I dunno, your average cute dude."

"Call Mrs. Miller for me, please," Leilani managed to eke out, but it felt like her world was condensing down to a tiny black spot. No, no, *no*, she was wrong. That couldn't be happening.

"Wait, what?"

"Call Mrs. Miller for me right *now*, please!"

"Oh geez, alright. Hold on."

Frenchie did as she asked, pressing a couple of buttons before handing the phone to Leilani.

"Oh Frenchie, did you find—"

"This is Leilani, but don't say my name. Please. In fact, just act like you're still talking to Frenchie and she can't find me."

To the woman's credit, there was only the slightest beat of a pause. "No, I'm not sure of her schedule. Did you check the barns, Frenchie?"

"Thank you. The men with you, can you tell me their names? Did they introduce themselves? *Don't* ask them if they haven't. They'll get suspicious."

"Oh, don't you worry about me, Kai, Bane and Philando are just so charming! They're telling me about surfing back home. Think I stand a chance on a boogie board?"

No.

Oh *no.*

Leilani realized she wasn't breathing, and that she definitely needed to draw in air, but she couldn't. Because after finally thinking she was safe, *he* was here.

He'd found her.

And she'd brought him right to some of the nicest people she knew.

"Mrs. Miller, I need you to listen very carefully," she wheezed when she could finally take in a rattling gasp. "Keep pretending everything is fine but get out of the home. Find any of your sons, but do not be alone with those three men. If you have any security, call them. Text the police too. You can do that silently. But I need you to get away from them *right* now."

"What? No, I don't know where you left the keys to the golf cart. Did you check out by the hydrangeas? I know I sometimes leave them on that one—you know what, I'll go look myself." The woman's voice grew faint for a moment. "I'll be right back, young men! Make yourselves at home!"

Thank goodness that Mrs. Miller had a cool head. There was some more pleasant, one-sided chitchat from the fake conversation the older woman was carrying on until, after what seemed like an eon, Leilani heard a deeper voice talk to her.

"Mom, you okay?"

It was one of the Miller boys. Leilani couldn't tell who, but that didn't matter. Mrs. Miller was safe, so now she could run.

She hung up and tossed the phone to Frenchie, her hands shaking from the cold shock of terror running through her.

"Those aren't your cousins, are they?" Frenchie asked in a small voice.

Leilani shook her head, trying to put her words together. But it was her worst nightmare shoved right in her face, the shadow that had been haunting her since she was seventeen years old looming again, making her feel so small and powerless.

"I'm sorry," she gasped, getting her body in order enough to scramble down the hay bale. She needed to run. She needed to *run* and yet it felt like her body was moving through mud. Where was her drive to survive and get away from danger? "Tell them that I won't be back. And I'm sorry."

Frenchie opened her mouth, but Leilani finally got her body to move, dashing as fast as she could to the employee parking lot.

She was breathless and sweaty by the time she reached it, but she didn't care. Once her trembling hands managed to pull her keys from the pocket and hit the unlock button on the fob, she practically threw herself in and peeled out like a madwoman.

But before she got to the long drive that led out, she thought better of it and pulled a sharp turn onto one of the service roads for workers. It wound around in the opposite direction, but it deposited her on a patch of road that was only about ten minutes from the interstate if she sped.

And she sped.

The interstate was *not* a direct route home. In fact, it added about twenty minutes and charged a toll, but she didn't think about it. She didn't think about any of it—other than making sure that they wouldn't know which direction she lived if they'd had someone set up to watch which direction she turned.

She didn't go home, either. Instead she drove to the last haven she had, parking her car behind the house and rushing up to Auntie Kini's porch where she knocked urgently. In the two minutes it took for the older woman to open the door, Leilani thought she might explode then and there. Thankfully, there was no spontaneous human combustion before her auntie pulled open the door.

"Oh, Leilani, what—"

But she was already throwing herself forward into the house. She stumbled, sinking to her knees and letting out the fearful, terrified sob that had been building in her chest for the entire drive.

"Sweetie, what's wrong?" Auntie Kini said, hurrying over to her.

Leilani just threw her arms and hugged the smaller woman around her waist, clinging to her like the last lifeline in choppy oceans.

"He's found me, Auntie Kini," she said between sobs, her world continuing to crumble away under her feet. "He's found me again."

9

———————

Simon

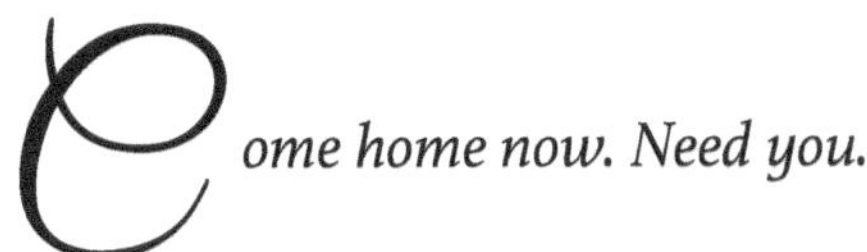 *ome home now. Need you.*

SIMON BLINKED AT HIS PHONE. It had buzzed while he was walking a familiar trail, enjoying the shade just as the afternoon sun was starting to really show off, so it was at least fifteen minutes later that he actually looked at the thing.

He'd been surprised to see it was his mom who texted him. She'd never been one for messaging when she could call, and her message wasn't like her either. His mom rarely ever asked for anything and she'd certainly never said she *needed* him.

So Simon turned around right then and there and rushed to his car.

At first he did try to pack up neatly and respect the

belongings, but the more seconds that passed, the more an uneasy feeling twisted in his gut. Eventually he just ripped everything up from the ground that he could, threw it into the back of his truck, and then secured the cover so he could race home.

He pressed the speed limit for most of the drive, worried about what he might find. He figured it couldn't be catastrophic because then one of his brothers definitely would have texted him too, but his mind was plagued with horrific ideas.

What if Mom fell down the stairs? What if Dad had suddenly died? Or if there was an employee accident. A fire? But all of those seemed too severe for just a text.

And his mom said she *needed* him. What could make his mom, one of the strongest and most patient women he knew, admit that she needed him?

He didn't know, but he aimed to find out.

Yet, as resolved as Simon was, he certainly wasn't expecting to pull up to the front of the estate and have it look like a tornado had blown through.

The front had several smashed windows, and it looked like things had been thrown onto the lawn. Mom's carefully manicured front was trampled. One of the front doors was hanging on by a hinge. Simon didn't even bother to turn off his truck, just throwing it into park before racing inside.

The inside was even worse. The foyer was *wrecked*, debris and mess everywhere, with almost all of the furniture either torn up, smashed or toppled over.

And for the first time in his life, Simon knew real fear.

"*MOM!*" he cried, feeling like his heart had stopped in his chest. If anything had happened to her... he would...

"In here," a voice answered that was definitely not his mom, but his brother. Fearing the worst, Simon dashed forward into their entertaining area where he found the source of the answer.

"Hey there," Sal said with exhaustion layering his tone. The giant man had a wicked black eye and was covered in a white dust that had to be either drywall or flour, some of it formed into little rivulets that had followed the sweat from his hairline.

"What happened here?" Simon asked, eyes wide as he looked past his giant brother.

Silas was sitting at one of the reading nooks built into the tall windows, Teddy holding a pack of frozen peas to his cheek. He looked much worse than Sal, with a busted lip, a cut across his nose, and some serious bruising peeking out from under the produce. As for Teddy, her knuckles were bloody and scabbing with what looked like a deep nail mark down one of her arms but was otherwise unharmed.

"Where's Mom?" Simon heard himself ask more desperately than he had intended.

What had happened?! Why were his brothers beat up? Had someone tried to rob them? Had someone *laid hands on his mom*?

Simon felt his anger, white-hot and raring, lick up his back and roast his brain. He didn't know what he'd do if someone had dared to harm his mom, and he didn't have a chance to figure it out before Sal calmly answered him.

"She's just in the bathroom. She wanted to wash her face and get the first aid kit. Don't worry; we didn't let them even get close to her."

It was like someone had taken all the wind out of him at once. Simon deflated, but at the same time couldn't help but be immensely relieved.

"Them? Who's them? Did you call the cops? Are they still around?"

"Whoa, one at a time," Sal said with a wry grin that looked like it was supposed to be humorous but a tone that didn't quite get there.

"The police were called before anything went down," Silas mumbled around his fat lip. "Leilani tipped her off. The police have already come and gone and taken pictures of everything and our statements."

That was a lot of information all at once and about a dozen questions all popped into his mind.

"Leilani? Is she okay? How long ago did this happen?" Their manor was an hour from the city, give or take, so even if the cops sped all the way to the estate with their sirens going, it had to have taken them at least forty minutes to arrive. Simon hadn't been *that* late in answering the text, so how long had they waited to contact him?

"Hey, it's okay. It was about three hours ago, maybe. We were giving statements and having the medics look everyone over, so we didn't text you right away. But everyone's been called back home, right now, you're just the first to arrive."

Okay, that made sense. But it still didn't make Simon feel any better. His family had been put in danger while he'd been off in the woods, trying to find something to maybe make himself feel a little less adrift. How *selfish* was that?

"Here, come sit down and hold this for me, will you?" Teddy said, holding out her hand to him.

He took it, allowing her to guide him to sit next to his brother and hold the significantly less frozen peas up to Silas's cheek.

"Here's what happened, as far as I can tell. Three men came here looking for Leilani, who split in a real hurry after warning your mother to get out and find help. Once they realized that they'd been duped, they tore up the entire kitchen.

"Your mom was completely safe. She'd managed to find Sal first, who called the police and took her to the employee building, where he had the shift supervisor call in a lockdown. Unfortunately, Silas's phone was dead, so he had no idea what was going on. And I had mine in the pocket of my overalls—that I'd just changed out of since I spilled windshield wiper fluid down my front after replacing fluids on all your trucks. So we walked right into what was happening.

"Naturally, we got into a scuffle, and Sal—who was coming back from making sure your mom was safe with the employees—rushed to join in."

Simon sat there, listening to it all. It sounded impossible, like something out of some action movie and not his life. And yet the evidence was right in front of him, impossible to ignore.

"Is Leilani alright?"

"We don't know."

"You don't *know*?" Simon countered, but then a door down the hall was opening and he saw it was Mom exiting from one of the bathrooms, her arms full of supplies.

"*Simon*," she said when she saw him. "You're here. Good. You still remember your Boy Scout first aid training?"

"I do," he answered, shifting the impromptu icepack to his other hand. "Why didn't any of you go with the paramedics if they were here?"

"Thankfully none of us are seriously hurt," his mom countered, calmly walking forward and setting her supplies out.

Simon could tell from the gentle lavender scent of their bathroom soap that she had definitely washed her hands and it looked like her face too. It took him back to times when he and his brothers had been banged up and she'd had particular rituals that came to playing nurse for them. Wash hands, arms, and face. Put on gloves. Tell terrible puns while examining wounds... The only time he could remember her abandoning that order was when Sterling had accidentally set off a firework in Silas's face, resulting in some pretty terrible burns that had permanently scarred him.

It made him feel better that his brothers were going to be treated and comforted in a way that only a mom knew how to do, but his mind flicked back to Leilani. Was she alright? Was she hurt? Was there someone to take care of her?

As if life heard his questions, a familiar little shape hurried in through the front door and a disheveled Frenchie was trotting toward them.

"I checked the security footage and confirmed she took off *asap*. She said she was sorry, and I think something about never meaning to cause us trouble, but Leilani is definitely long gone."

Cold dread filled Simon's stomach, sharp and crisp. "Where did she go?"

"Well, home I assume. Even if she's planning on skipping town, she's got a place so she'll need to grab things." Frenchie clicked her tongue and shook her head. "I remember what it was like to have to get out of somewhere in a hurry, though. Are we sure we did the right thing about not telling the cops about her? I don't entirely trust them either but... I'm worried."

"You didn't tell the cops about Leilani?" Simon asked incredulously, nearly dropping the ice pack.

"No, we didn't," his mom said coolly, sitting Sal down and looking him over for cuts and bruises.

"Why not?"

"I learned it from your aunt, actually, after an incident she had with Bradley's young wife. We gave the cops all the information we had about the three and where we saw them leave, but we wait until we talk to Leilani directly before we give them any information about her. For her protection."

Simon had no idea how that could be for Leilani's protection, but his mom's tone said there was no arguing with her, so he slid right on past that point.

"Does anyone know her address?"

Frenchie shook her head. "I know she was getting ready to upgrade her apartment since she's in a studio right now, but that's about it."

Drat. Simon chewed at his lip a moment before his brain practically sparked. "What about her onboarding paperwork? It has to be there, or in the system, right?"

He looked to Silas hopefully, waiting for his brother to have the same epiphany moment, but he just frowned around his swollen lip. "That's illegal."

"Pardon?"

"Leilani's left, effectively quitting, and we have no right to use her address for anything except sending her the termination packet that outlines what she can do with her benefits and a paystub. Giving it to you for you to go there would be a huge breach of privacy."

There was that temper again, roiling up inside of him and ready to spit. Leilani needed help and his brother was quibbling over *red tape* with him! It was a waste of time when Simon could be out the door already.

"Breach of privacy? Are you *kidding* me?"

"No, I'm not. Look, I know you hired her and liked to stare after her like a lost puppy, but clearly Leilani had some things that she didn't feel comfortable sharing with us. That doesn't give us a right to just barge into her personal dwelling—"

Before Simon could even argue with his older brother, a gentle hand rested on Silas's shoulder.

"Honey, I know you're trying to do what's right, but I think that these are extenuating circumstances." Teddy's voice was softer than Simon had ever heard it and the expression on her face was gently loving. He didn't think he'd ever had anyone look at him like *that*. It was beginning to make sense how she'd completely changed Silas's path. "Remember when we first met, and I was too scared, too angry to trust you? Leilani could be in a lot of danger, and we might be the only people who can help her. I think, in this case, it might be wise to take the risk and try to do something rather than sit back and hope."

Silas was quiet a moment, a long moment that made Simon want to rip out his own hair and yell at the sky. But he stayed quiet because—even if he often did look down on his family for being so stuck in their tiny worlds—he respected the man enough to let him think for a beat.

"Alright." Silas pushed Simon's hand and the ice pack away then stood. "I'll go to my office and email it. My phone's not on the protected server so I can't access it from here. You head to your truck and I'll message it to you, but I need you to delete it as soon as you plug it into your GPS, okay?"

"Yes, of course. Whatever you need." Simon was already up on his feet and racing out. Details all became a blur to him as he hopped into his truck and waited for the info. The moment he got it, he raced off, and every single minute of the ride was pure agony.

There were three men who wanted Leilani, and they were the type of guys to destroy a house and fight his siblings. And also Teddy, apparently, judging by the condition of her hands. He'd heard that the mechanic was not one to mess with in a fight, but he'd always figured those stories were exaggerated. Clearly, he was wrong. The woman obviously knew how to take care of herself.

But would Leilani? For the two months that she'd been on the ranch, Leilani hadn't raised her hand to anyone. She didn't walk with a defensive posture or even a guarded one. Sure, she was observably strong considering all the tasks that she could do, including the strenuous muckraking, but being strong and knowing how to fight were two different things.

What if those three men had found her? Cornered her? What if they *had* her? It was so outside of anything that Simon had ever had to think about that he could feel himself getting sick to his stomach with fear.

He couldn't say how long it took him to make it to the awful building that her studio room was apparently located, but he let himself in the completely unsecured front door and thundered up the steps to where her place was supposed to be located.

His heart practically leaped out of his throat when he saw her door was cracked open. He was too late. The first person that he'd clicked with in years was gone or hurt or—

Simon cut himself off and rushed in. He tried mentally steeling himself for what he might see, and yet he was still startled by a loud yelp at his entrance.

"I'm arm—*Simon*! What are you doing here!?"

It was Leilani. Beautiful, strong, scared-looking Leilani, standing in the kitchenette with a suitcase, duffle, and messenger bag around her.

He'd made it in time.

The relief that flooded through him almost made his knees give out, but he kept it together. Time was of the essence and he wanted, no, *needed* to get Leilani to safety.

He knew none of it made sense, but there was a deep, virulent force in him that was desperate to protect her. That wanted to see her laugh and smile and make sure nothing ever hurt her and no man ever laid hands on her again like that grabber at the bar. It was ridiculous. He didn't know her. He couldn't say what her favorite color was, if she was a cat or a dog person, or even anything about his family. And yet, it was there. Burning hotly within him. She *had* to be safe. She *had* to.

But before he could verbalize a single drop of that, Leilani was hurriedly speaking, her tone laced with fear and panic and everything he wanted to shield her from.

"I'm so, so sorry. I thought I was safe. I really did. I never would have accepted the job—would have put your family in danger if I thought they could find me. I *never* posted about it anywhere and only told my mom and aunt, so I don't understand how they found me. Please, please, understand I would never do that. Never!"

Her words were coming so fast that he could only pick out parts of it. But even if he couldn't make out all the mushed-up words, he could hear the terror behind them, and he hated it. He hated seeing her scared.

He also understood what all the bags around her implied, and his own panic was increasing. She was going to leave—to who knew where—and he would likely never see her again. He would have no way of knowing if she was safe, in danger, or if whatever vandals had attacked his family had found her.

And the thought made him sick. He *knew* he had no right to her; he knew that he was practically a stranger to her, but all that logic didn't stop his heart from pounding at the thought of her being alone and in danger.

"Please don't go," he said before he could think better of it. He hoped that she could hear the need in his voice but at the same time hoped that she couldn't. He didn't want her to think that he expected a "favor" for helping her, or that he had an ulterior motive. She could ignore him for the rest of his life and he'd live with it as long as she was safe.

"I don't have a choice," she answered back, breathless and voice small.

Simon had never heard her sound so defeated, so crumbled, and he ached to do something to fix it. That purposelessness that always haunted him disappeared, giving way to the *need* to take care of her.

"They already know where I work; it's only a matter of time before they find out where I live. I can't risk that. It's too easy to break in here and takes too long for cops to respond to this side of town."

"Then move in with us!" Impossible. Ludicrous, and yet it shone in his mind as a blazing possibility. The *only* possibility. Leilani would be close and surrounded by his brothers and on their property. Considering everything that happened, he very much doubted that the men who ransacked the kitchen would be coming back again. "We have plenty of room. We have whole floors open!"

Plus, they could hire some security guards. They'd gotten lax, having only a handful of night workers who generally patrolled and maintained things, but his family could hire a dozen more in the blink of an eye.

So maybe not impossible or ludicrous, but the way Leilani was staring at him certainly made it out that she thought as much.

"I... what about Auntie Kini? I was going to take her too, a road trip of sorts. She would come back in a month or so, when it's safe, but only then."

"She can stay too! Both of you can share a room or have separate rooms, even separate wings if you want. And you can both stay as long as you need. A month. Two months. Six? I don't care. Whatever keeps you safe."

"I..." She stopped herself, taking a moment to swallow then looking down at the bags surrounding her.

Simon wanted to beg, to plead with her, but he knew she needed to come to a decision on her own.

Leilani didn't move. "How are you able to offer out these big, grand things when I haven't done a single thing to earn your trust? I don't understand."

Now it was his turn to sputter out, not sure what to say. "I'm, uh..."

"Do you want something from me? Have you been playing some sort of strange long game? Because I've never been much on dating since everything happened with Kai. I'm saving myself for someone who makes me feel safe, and right now, I don't think that person exists."

"No, no, I don't want anything from you. I'm not trying to hold this over your head for anything. I just want to do what's right. I just want you safe."

"That doesn't make sense. No one does these kinds of things for nothing."

"I know," Simon answered honestly, hoping she could hear how genuinely he meant every word he said. "And yet that's why. I just want to see you protected and able to live your life. That's it."

"You've got to know how insane that sounds."

"Oh, believe me, I do."

10

Leilani

"$\mathcal{H}$ere, let me help you—"

"Oh, that's alright, Miss Leilani, I've got a hand on it."

Leilani pulled back and watched skeptically as Sterling balanced two of her totes right on top of each other while headed inside. She didn't have much, enough to fill her car and Simon's truck. Auntie Kini had even less, barely filling out Sal's truck. She kept trying to help carry things up the stairs where they would be staying in Samuel's smallest addition (which wasn't small at all—great mahi-mahi, rich people were *wild*), but the Miller brothers kept insisting on doing all the physical labor themselves while having her direct them. Between that and Mrs. Miller peppering the both of them with food and drinks, the entire move-in process was over before she knew it and all their stuff was in adjacent rooms.

Standing in the doorway, looking at her totes and bags carefully stacked against the edge of a bedroom that was bigger than her whole studio apartment, she couldn't help but feel like she was still in shock from everything that had happened. And also scared. And maybe... just maybe a little hopeful too.

Nobody had asked her the full story of what had happened. No one grilled her on who those men were and why they wanted her. It was lovely but surprising, and once more entirely too trusting. How did they know she was one of the good ones?

They didn't, and yet they still welcomed her with open arms. Amazing.

It didn't seem real, and yet there she was, standing in a place that was temporarily *her* room, while the Miller brothers had left her alone to give her space and go shower off the grime from helping her move.

She called her mom, of course. She would have included Auntie Kini, but the woman was downstairs with Mrs. Miller, enjoying tea and crackers together while no doubt discussing what had happened. The only one who really had no idea what was going on was her mother, but everything had been such a whirlwind that Leilani hadn't had time to update her.

It seemed impossible to believe that just four hours earlier, she'd been shoving her most precious items into bags so she could flee the state. But the Millers worked fast and the next thing she knew, after agreeing to Simon's blurted offer, four of the six brothers were in her studio and packing things for her, then hauling them down the several flights of stairs.

Sitting on the edge of the bed that was now hers for the near future, Leilani dialed up her mother for a video chat.

"Aloha, my—what is going on?"

"I didn't even say anything yet, Mom."

"I know that face. It's one I don't like to see. What has happened? Did those rich folks turn out to be racist?"

"What? No, Mom, they're amazing. Beyond amazing, even."

"*Oooh*, does this mean maybe you have opened your eyes about dating one of these rich young ranchers?"

"*MOM!* No. They're almost all taken anyway."

"Almost doesn't mean all, my love."

Leilani took a deep breath and decided to just get the words out. Although she was twenty-three years old as of a couple weeks ago, her mother did still have a knack for steamrolling her about her romantic life.

But her mom continued, "I'm just saying, if they're beyond nice and they like taking care of you *and* very handsome, I don't see why—"

"Kai found me."

Her mother's face froze, then there was a flurry of movement. Leilani realized that she was getting up from where she'd been sitting on the couch to go to her room, where she closed the door.

"What happened?"

"He didn't see me, but he went to my job. I don't know how he found out where I was, but he did. The cops are after him, and this time, since it was rich people's stuff he's messed with, I'm hoping he'll be driven out of the state."

"But still, *Texas*? I never would have sent you if I thought..." Her mother let out a long, pained sighed. "Are you alright? Where are you now? Safe? I assume that's why you're calling."

"Yeah. I'm safe. I'm actually staying with the Millers right now."

"Wait, with the rich family? In their *mansion?*"

"Mom, this is like a mansion's mansion. I feel like other

mansions look at this place and wish they could be like it when they grow up."

"*Shoot*. That's something. At least there's some upside to all of this."

"Yeah, it's definitely an upside." Suddenly, Leilani was antsy. Her day had gone from warm and pleasant to terrifying to amazing all in a very short time. She was exhausted, but the last vestiges of adrenaline were pumping through her, making her want to get up and move like she was still being hunted. "Hey, do you want a tour? I bet Mrs. Miller would love to meet you, and Auntie Kini is here too."

"Those *haoles* invited Auntie to stay too? You weren't kidding about them being nice, were you?"

"Not something I would kid about in this day and age."

"Hah! I hear that. Alright, take me on a tour, honey."

Leilani smiled, her feelings simmering down somewhat. She was in a serious situation, a scary situation, but it felt easier to believe that it might somehow work itself out with her mother smiling at her on the other side of her phone screen.

At one point in the tour, she must have gotten turned around, because instead of ending up back at her room or even at the start of Silas's hall, she ended up in front of the center stair down to the main foyer. That was odd considering that she'd taken the left-hand curved stairwell to get up to her room, but it seemed that the Miller estate was also partially a maze.

"Are you telling me you got lost in a *house*?" her mom tittered, barely trying to suppress her laughter.

"Hey, you would too," Leilani countered, headed toward the stairs only to pull up short when an unfamiliar figure stepped out of the set of ornate double doors that led into what she believed was the master wing.

Leilani startled, her mind instantly going to Kai and his buddies, but she managed to stop herself from running away long enough to realize that it was an older and very much white gentleman.

Oh! It must have been Mr. Miller who she'd read about. She could only barely remember his picture, but the man in front of her seemed to match up well enough.

"Whoa, sorry there. I got a little—"

"Who are you?"

Right! Where were her manners? Leilani extended her hand, giving him one of her charming grins that she knew usually had people melting right away. "Hi, my name's Leilani. I want to say thank you again for everything—"

But the man let out such a derisive huff that she stopped mid-sentence.

"I couldn't care which of my sons you're laying about with. Try to dredge up what little respect you've been taught and pick things off from their areas of my home, not mine."

Now Leilani did believe in respecting her elders. She also believed in being grateful for any and all gifts. But what she didn't believe in, was being talked down to or maligned for absolutely no reason.

"Excuse you, *sir*, but I am not involved with any of your sons. I am an employee of yours and my aunt is a friend of your wife's. I apologize for infringing on your personal space, but I was simply turned around while showing my mother your lovely home. I do not appreciate your insinuations about my character, and I would appreciate it if you would apologize."

The man turned redder, and she had the feeling that was the wrong thing to say to appease him, but oh well. She'd worked for too long as a waitress to worry about holding her tongue when someone was being blatantly impolite to her.

"Apologize? You think I don't see through you? All the others were 'just workers' too. You think you're any different? I'm not an idiot. We let one of you in and now you're all scuttling, trying to find a place where you can latch on and feed off my hard work."

Wow. *Wow.* Of course, Leilani had seen videos of entitled older folks online. She'd made the occasional Boomer joke. But never in her life did she think she would meet one in the flesh.

She didn't answer him for a moment, locking her eyes on him and giving him the most amused glance she could. He was a couple of inches taller than her, but that didn't matter. "I know that you're used to a life of everyone bowing to your every whim, but let me tell you, that's *not* going to happen here."

"You think you can tell me what to do in my own—"

"I am not telling you what to do," Leilani cut in calmly. She had to show him that he didn't get under her skin. That he was silly and wasting his energy like a child throwing a tantrum. "I am informing you of how I will be treated. I love my position and am incredibly grateful to your family for changing my life. But that does not give you purview—"

The man was almost crimson. "Listen here, you wet—"

His words were cut off by the sound of a door hitting a wall, and suddenly Simon was striding toward them from a different hall. For a moment, just the *briefest* of moments, her stomach sank as she was sure that he was going to take his dad's side and berate her. But he didn't do anything of the sort. Instead he whirled on the shorter man, his own face mirroring the anger there.

"What in the name of all good do you think you're doing, Dad?"

"Don't you talk to me like—"

"Don't *you* talk to our guest like that! I heard you all the way down to my room! What are you *thinking*?"

"Oh, so she's yours then, huh? You decide to play in the trash like all of your—"

"Don't you *dare* finish that sentence, Dad. Do whatever you were going to do and move on. Leilani is an innocent party in all of this. You're making a donkey out of yourself."

"A donkey, huh? *I'm* the donkey when the lot of you are lowering yourself to streetwalkers and janitors?"

"Do you even *hear* yourself? How can you talk like that about your future daughters-in-law? About the women that your sons love!"

Leilani watched the two of them blow up at each other, turning away to look at her mom, who had very clearly heard everything.

"Ah, there it is. I knew they were too good to be true. Be careful, Leilani, a lot of mainlanders don't have the same idea of family as we do."

"I understand, Mom. Thanks. I'll talk to you later."

"Aloha, my love."

"Aloha."

When Leilani turned back, Simon and his dad were still yelling at each other, voices rising in volume with each shout. She had no idea why Simon was going to bat so hard for her. He didn't know her and that was his own *dad.* And yet... it really seemed like he cared about her in a way that didn't make sense.

She would get it if he'd shown any interest in her since that first meeting, or if he'd tried to date her or even be a friend to her. But he always avoided her or treated her with kid gloves. She felt like the closest thing she had to a real interaction with him was when he begged her not to go.

It was probably indicative of her damage that seeing him shout at someone, red in the cheeks and brows furrowed, made her heart warm. But it did. He was standing up for her at his own detriment. Folks didn't do that often, and certainly not for random women from diners.

Still, as much as it made her feel nice that he was defending her, she felt like she should break up the fight rather than let it escalate. But she didn't quite know how, and she worried that stepping in would cross a boundary that she shouldn't as a guest.

But all that was solved when a loud and firm decree came from the bottom of the stairs.

"McLintoc Darragh Miller, what on earth are you doing?"

They all turned at once to see Mrs. Miller standing at the foot of the main stair, looking up with the stern but contained sort of anger that a *very* unhappy mother could exude.

"Your son—"

"*Our* son came up to ask *my* guest to dinner now that it's ready. *You* will be returning to your room to cool down and go over our evening devotional, won't you?"

"I—"

"I am not sure you understood what I meant, *McLintoc.* Should I repeat myself?"

Leilani wasn't sure what she expected, but it wasn't for the rage on the man's face to slowly fizzle out until he just looked exhausted.

"No. I *am* behind on the devotional. I'll go catch up if you want to send dinner up."

"The staff have gone home today because of the *incident* your medication had you nap through. I will bring you supper when our guests have been tended to."

"I see."

"Oh, and husband?"

"Yes, wife?"

"Apologize to our lovely guest for being so unpleasant in front of her."

That red started to return again and he huffed in a great breath as if he were going to argue, but Mrs. Miller just leveled him with the most mom-glare she had ever seen, and her own mother had given her a doozie of a one when she'd caught Leilani trying to climb a palm tree with nothing but a pillowcase.

"Apologies for the misunderstanding," Mr. Miller said gruffly, not even looking her in the eye. "I mistook you for someone else."

If it were another situation, Leilani would have countered with who, as it was a clear cop-out, but she just wanted the situation to *end*. Sure, it wasn't the high-stakes drama she had going on with Kai, but it was plenty uncomfortable.

Besides, she wanted to examine the warm and fuzzies that were still churning in her gut over Simon defending her so stalwartly. That definitely felt pretty concerning.

"I appreciate your apology. I look forward to getting to know each other better."

He gave the slightest of nods then whipped around, heading off as fast as a gentleman of his age could while still being dignified. The double doors slammed after him, but there was still a Mr. Miller shaped void of awkwardness left behind.

"Leilani, my sweet, I understand it's been a long day. Would you like it if I brought dinner up for you and your lovely aunt to have together and recoup rather than downstairs in our stuffy dining room?"

Leilani almost sagged with relief. "Yes, I would absolutely love that. Thank you for understanding, Mrs. Miller."

"Of course, my dear. I know plenty about stress! Simon, be a love and show her the way back to her room? She's not our first guest to get lost."

Simon tilted his head in agreement, his lips still pressed in a thin line and his chest rising and falling faster than it should have for a resting rate of breathing. *And what a chest it was.* Leilani always tried to avoid ogling her bosses, but she could see the taut muscles of his frame moving as he breathed, and it was hard *not* to notice the stern cut of him.

Mom was right, of course. He was handsome. She'd always known that, but it was the first moment where it actually seemed to matter.

...that was also very much concerning.

"Alright, it'll be just a few minutes, Leilani. You get settled in and I'll be right up. I want you to be happy and comfortable here, okay? You're welcome in my home from the very bottom of my heart."

"Thanks, Mrs. Miller. I owe so much to you."

"Nonsense. This is just what family does. Head along now."

Leilani nodded and looked to Simon, who walked back the way she should have come. This time, as they walked along, he pointed out "landmarks" that could help her if she got mixed-up. Apparently, the same thing had happened to Elizabeth a couple times and even Nova once, back when Mom had been redecorating the bathroom closest to the kitchen and sent the woman to the second-floor storage closet to get the doilies she wanted.

It didn't take long to make it to her door and Leilani felt like she *should* say something, but she had no idea what.

Thanks for yelling at your dad for me?

Why do you care so much?

Why do you look at me like that *sometimes when you say you don't want anything from me?*

Instead, it was Simon who spoke first. "So, what's going on?"

"Huh?" She had been so wrapped up in her own thoughts that she didn't quite catch his meaning.

"Who were those three men? Why were they after you? And why were they so angry? Are they trying to hurt you?"

Oh. Of course, he would want to know what was happening. He'd opened his home to her and defended her from his own father. Surely, he was owed an explanation.

And yet it wasn't an explanation that came out of her mouth.

"It's nothing. I just... I really owe you and your family everything for giving us a place to stay while the cops are looking for them."

He didn't answer right away, giving her a long look that let her know that her "nothing" wasn't convincing at all. But he didn't press her, and as the seconds ticked by, eventually he gave her a sad sort of nod.

"You don't owe us a thing. But I do hope that maybe one day you'll trust me enough to tell me the story. Have a good night, Miss Leilani."

Yet another tip of his head and then he was walking off down the hall, leaving Leilani standing in front of her door.

Oh.

11

───────

Simon

*L*iving with Leilani in the house was both great and awful simultaneously. He was closer to her, able to watch out for her and know she was safe, but at the same time she kept insisting on working and acting like everything was normal, which made it ever so hard to *protect* her.

She insisted on helping the paid contractors clean things up, which put her far too close to the windows. And after the general cleanup was done in a couple days and expert tradesmen came in to make repairs, she went outside and tried to keep up on her work.

Simon didn't want to tell her what to do—he *didn't*. But he didn't understand how she could be so glib when three men who were willing to wreck a house had popped up out of nowhere and asked for her. Men who scared her enough to make her flee the state she was from. And yet she was out and about, trying to muckrake, take care of the baby goats, and even socialize the pigs.

He could tell he was grating on her nerves, but it wasn't like he could stop. He always tried to keep his distance, but by the fourth day, he wasn't surprised when she came storming out of the horse barn with her full lips pressed firmly together.

"Would you *please* just stop watching me like I'm a toddler who's going to hurt themselves?" she asked, looking up where he was perched on top of a hay bale, with a couple of the horses idly gazing below him.

He figured if he did a couple of chores while he kept on the lookout, it would be much more productive and less creepy than if he was just staring at Leilani.

"I'm not watching *you*," Simon countered calmly. "I'm making sure those lowlifes don't come back."

Leilani huffed, but he didn't miss the color that spread across her cheeks, even from where he was sitting. "Look, you've done a ton for me, but I really don't do well with feeling like I'm being watched. That's how *he* got started and it just... it makes me feel real bad, okay?"

"He who?"

She closed her eyes and took a deep breath. "Kai. The leader. Guy with the long hair."

"I... I'm not sure I understand what you mean. He watched you?"

"Look, it's not for you to understand. You offering your home to me has been an immense kindness, really. But you can't hold it over my head as an excuse to stalk me. I need space. I need you to not be looking at me all the time, even if you mean well."

Stalk her? Was that what it seemed like? That was about as unflattering as anything. Simon had to swallow hard.

"Look Leilani—"

"I don't want to hear it. I don't. Thank you for everything, *really*, but leave me alone. While I'm trying to work, alright? Please, that's all I ask."

He couldn't even get so much as another word in before she walked off, resolutely shutting the door of the horse barn.

Welp, the lady said what the lady said, and although he absolutely didn't want to, he clambered down the hay bale and headed back toward his truck. Part of him was screaming to stop, to go back and make sure that she was safe, that those three men could be hiding around any corner, and that there could be *more* of them.

But instead he respected her wishes.

Even if he really, *really* didn't want to.

"Hey, I'm about to run some supplies out to our adopted farm family, did you want to come with?"

Simon blinked and looked away from his computer, where he'd been refreshing his email to see if there was an update from the police officers handling their case. While the insurance had been plenty good at corresponding and estimates, the cops had been less fruitful in their search. It had been almost a full week and none of the three were in custody.

"Farm family?" Simon asked, trying to rub some moisture back into his eyes.

Sterling had a little smile on his face as he started telling Simon about the project they were working on. "Yeah, it's a new thing that Solomon and Samuel put together. They set up a sort of fund online for independent and small-scale farmers to apply to, and we help them with certain needs.

Solomon told me there's a family about, uh, I think it was about two hours away from here that could use a new coop and some compost, so me and a couple of the workers are taking a bunch of stuff down that will save them a pretty penny."

"We have an online fund now?"

"Oh yeah, we have all sorts of things. I know I've been pretty centered on the soil and the animals, but Solomon, Silas and Sal have been focusing on either the business or the city. Although I'm pretty sure this was Samuel's idea. Of course, Dad doesn't know about it, which is probably for the best."

Yeah, it was. If Mr. Miller knew that his heir apparent was running a charity with the son that left the estate, he'd be more than livid.

"You need help packing up the truck?"

"Nah, we got that, and the trailer already loaded. I just figured maybe you'd wanna ride along. See what we're up to. Maybe get out of Leilani's hair before you make her hate you."

Simon grimaced. "You heard about that, huh?"

"I may have overheard some complainin' she did to Nova. But don't worry, she knows you mean well and so do we. You just have to trust our security team and our workers, okay? Nobody's going to snatch her up in broad daylight now that all of us know who they are. That lot rolled up pro'bly thinking that Leilani would go quietly with them rather than risk trouble."

"She would have," Simon said with absolute certainty. "If they were able to get her while only Mom and Frenchie were around, she would never have risked their safety."

"I think you're right on that. Anyway, ya in or out?"

It was the first time in years he'd been asked to pitch in on a project with his brothers, so he found himself standing up and grabbing one of the hats he hung by the door. "You know, that sounds like a good idea."

"Great! It'll certainly make things go faster. I'm glad to have you."

And Simon was glad to be wanted. Once more, that void in his chest shrunk just a bit further. Maybe it would be too much to hope for, but it almost felt like he was finding a direction.

Too bad that direction seemed to be mostly taking him toward a mysterious woman who he was driving up the wall.

SIMON HEADED INTO THE KITCHEN, bleary-eyed from the rare nap he had taken after Sterling had kept him up late explaining about his soil experiments while they watched old Westerns. He knew better than to try to keep to the twin's schedule, as Sterling had always been a peculiar sleeper. He usually passed out around ten or so, then woke up from two a.m. until sometime around six or eight and then slept until noon. He'd been to all sorts of doctors to fix it when he was a teen, but it just seemed that his circadian rhythm was locked into the primitive habit of waking in the middle of the night.

He was so out of it that he didn't even hear voices coming from the kitchen until he was standing in the doorway, looking over Mom and Auntie Kini, who were at the stove, while Leilani, Nova and Elizabeth all sat at the newly refurbished island bar.

The contractors had really done a good job. It had only been a week and one day, yet the kitchen wasn't just good as new, but better. They'd redone some of the lighting, made things more energy-efficient, built better shelving, and even had a rotating sort of organization system in one of the side pantries. The stools were wider yet somehow sleeker looking, and tall enough to handle the long legs that many of the occupants of the kitchen had. There were even a couple of shorter ones at the kitchen counter, no doubt meant for Mom, Frenchie, and Auntie Kini.

"Oh, hello there, young man," Auntie Kini said, beckoning him over with a waving hand. "I was just going to teach all of you how to make spam musubi!"

"Spam what now?" he asked, his peripheral vision subconsciously flicking to Leilani. She looked as good as usual, dressed casually on her day off, while he felt like he looked akin to something that crawled off the bottom of a shoe. His hair was mussed, his eyes were bleary, and he was in his sleep clothes.

"Spam musubi," Auntie Kini repeated. "Perhaps one of the best snacks in the world."

"I think maybe you might be a little biased, Auntie," Leilani said with amusement.

"And I think last time I made these you ate six in a row."

"I didn't say I wasn't biased either."

There was a laugh all around, except for Simon, who crossed to the cabinets to grab a cup, then to the fridge to get some water. He could at least be hydrated if he was getting pulled into some sort of group activity.

"I've always wanted to learn how to roll sushi," Nova said, clapping her hands. "They made a spam dish in Guam that was just like... super greasy so I was never into it, but if this is supposed to be a handheld thing, then it can't be drippy, right?"

"Right, spam musubi isn't drippy," Leilani said, patting her friend on the back.

Nova rolled her eyes and elbowed her, leaving the two to

play fight until Elizabeth started placing fake bets with the almonds they were snacking on.

"Alright, settle down. I'm bringing over the spam. Leilani, will you see if the rice is done cooling in the fridge?"

"Sure," she said, making a cute little curtsy when she got off her chair.

Simon stepped out of her way as she withdrew a tray of rice that had been mostly pressed flat onto a tray. It smelled nice, but there was something strange to it. Something he wasn't used to.

"Why does that smell different?"

"Sushi vinegar," she answered with a smile. "Touch'a sugar too. Gives it depth and cuts the salt and fat of the spam."

"Huh."

He watched as she set it on the island, then laid out three small bamboo mats that he recognized from a couple of sushi places he'd gone to.

"Where's the nori, Auntie?"

"Should be in my bag that I set by the pantry. I brought all the essentials we would need." Her eyes flicked to Mrs. Miller. "No offense meant, of course. But I wasn't certain if you would have the supplies for some of my favorite foods."

"None taken, don't worry. I'm so excited to try something new. You know, it's not every day you get to make and cook something you've never heard of."

"This is very true," Auntie Kini said gravely. "That is why you are a wise woman."

"Hah, stop it, you. You're already in my house, so you don't need to butter me up."

"Now that is a lie. One can never have too much butter." Auntie Kini winked.

The two older women continued to joke with each other,

throwing compliments back and forth while Leilani retrieved a packet of what looked like dark green, shiny paper. Opening it up, she took out the sheets one by one and waved them over a hot burner, then set it in front of Nova, Elizabeth, and on an empty plate he assumed was reserved for his mother.

"Well," Leilani said, shooting him a glance over her shoulder. "Are you coming?"

Simon said nothing for a beat, then his mind kicked in and told him that she was talking to him. "Wait, me? You want me to make spammusi... spam..."

"Spam musubi. And only if you want to. This is not compulsory."

Simon swallowed, wondering if she could tell how his heart's tempo just picked up. "Sure. I'm game."

He walked over to the empty plate and watched as Leilani put the green paper on top of the bamboo rolling mat.

"This is nori. It goes on the outside of the musubi. Now, you take your rice scoopy and spread the rice out thinly—but not too thinly—over the sheet. Make sure you leave enough at the top blank so you can roll it properly. As for the nori, it goes shiny side down."

She walked them through it carefully, seeming to enjoy herself and never being annoyed when she had to repeat things or if one of them wanted her to stand by and watch to make sure they didn't mess up. Elizabeth was particularly needy, which was surprising, and asked Leilani every step of the way to make sure she was doing it correctly.

Then again, after hearing Sterling talk about her work drive and perfectionist streak, maybe that wasn't so surprising.

He did alright himself. It didn't look as neat or as uniform as Leilani's (which she'd done in less than a minute, it seemed), but it wasn't half bad. And he only tore one sheet of the nori—

which was apparently seaweed—as opposed to Nova, who tore three.

As for Mom and Auntie Kini, they seemed perfectly happy working together. Simon had never thought of it before, but he couldn't remember the last time he'd seen his mom hanging around with another woman her age. Or really hanging out with anyone who wasn't her sons or a fellow church member. Sure, she schmoozed with the best of them at parties, and attended plenty of charity functions, but did his mom have any *friends*?

He tried to think back. When they were kids, it seemed like she'd had a circle of gal-pals in the form of the moms of his and his brothers' friends. Not to mention mothers from the PTA.

But as he and his brothers had gotten older, those women seemed to have faded away, all off doing their own things. Even when he visited, his mom had mostly been on her own until her daughters-in-law started to filter in.

...was his mom lonely?

The thought surprised him far more than it probably should have. Maybe he would have lingered on it longer if Auntie Kini didn't come over with a piping hot plate of what looked like very thick-sliced bologna.

"What's this?" he asked, eyeing the stuff.

"It's *spam*," Elizabeth said like he was crazy.

"Oh, I didn't know. I don't think that I've ever seen spam before."

"You've never seen *spam*?" Somehow Leilani sounded offended, and he didn't quite get it. "Spam is the lifeblood of snackitude! It's salty, it's savory, it's filling! It is comfort food at its finest!"

"I definitely think you might be biased," Nova muttered, her tongue sticking out of the side of her mouth as she smoothed her rice for the fourth time.

"I'm not biased, I'm right," Leilani countered primly, tossing her braid over her shoulder dramatically.

"Of all my *ohana*, Leilani was always the most excited for the Waikiki Spam Jam," Auntie Kini murmured lovingly, reaching up to pinch at the young woman's cheeks.

Simon watched the whole scene with interest. Sure, he'd observed her having all sorts of fun and making people laugh from afar, but he'd never really been up in the proceedings. He liked them. Watching her was kind of like watching sunlight spill over his mom's garden. Warm and bright, but with a sort of invigorating undercurrent of knowing he was watching something positive that fueled growth.

"The what now?" Elizabeth asked, looking up from her meticulously flat rice-on-nori.

"The Waikiki Spam Jam," Leilani said with a broad grin. "It's magical."

"Yes, it is," Auntie Kini said. "But so is spam musubi, and if you don't stop daydreaming about home, then we're not going to finish teaching anyone how to make it."

"Which means we won't get to eat it," Mrs. Miller chimed in with faux horror. "We wouldn't want *that* would we?"

"Alright, alright. I get it. You guys, use your tongs to lay the spam all the way down at the bottom, lining it up with the edge of the rice. Yeah, there you go, easy peasy." They all did as she said fairly quickly, so she rolled right onto the next step while the older women were already off in their own conversation.

"Now, feel free to go as slow as you want, but now you use the bamboo mat to roll it. Like so." Leilani demonstrated, making it look so *easy*.

Simon had never made sushi or musubi or whatever a day

in his life, so he knew there was no way it was going to go that smoothly for him.

But he still tried.

It didn't really work the first time, or the second, and after that he stopped, waiting for Leilani to finish helping Nova. When she did, their eyes made contact and she flashed him a wry grin that reminded him of exactly why she'd caught his attention in the diner.

"Need some help there?"

"Definitely."

She came around to the other side of the island, leaning down and placing her hands over his, showing him where he needed to put them and how to hold the mat with one while using the other for rolling.

It wasn't quite someone teaching him to play pool behind his back like so many movies liked to do, but he got the same sort of rushing feeling that he was pretty sure those scenes were supposed to encourage. Suddenly he was acutely aware of all of Leilani. The scent of her perfume, the way her lashes half covered her eyes as she concentrated on their joined hands. How soft her skin was. He tried to keep his gaze only where it was respectful, but his peripheral vision still noticed the smooth curve of her, and just how womanly her frame was.

"Hey, tighten up your grip here. I promise you won't break it."

What?

Oh. Right. She was teaching him how to make her favorite snack. And maybe if he got good at making her favorite snack, he could bring it to her sometimes. That would be an excuse to hang out with her without her feeling like it was stalking.

Returning his concentration to the task at hand, he did as

she asked, and soon there was a mostly okay-looking roll of green in front of him.

"You did it!"

Simon hadn't realized how much he'd bent forward in his concentration until he glanced up at Leilani's praise. Suddenly their faces were so much closer to each other than they'd ever been, and his breath caught right in his throat.

Time seemed to freeze, just the two of them in each other's bubble, and his whole body seemed to go haywire. He could feel his palms start to sweat, his heart start to race, and his skin flush with warmth.

It would have been one thing if he was the only one affected. He could play it off in a sneeze or even joke. But one look at the expression on Leilani's face had him locked in the moment. Her eyes were half-lidded as they regarded him, full of a warm, hazy expression as they moved across his face. Her plush lips were open slightly, with the faintest breath rasping out of them. Even her golden, beautifully round cheeks were flushed slightly, the red accenting the flower she had tucked behind her ear.

"Oh! I got it!"

Elizabeth's elated cry had both of them jolting backward, the moment gone. But even with it over, Simon knew it was burned in his mind forever.

Because when Leilani looked at him, he felt seen. He felt centered and purposefully made in a way he had never felt before.

He could see himself getting addicted to that feeling.

Granted, the question was, did Leilani feel the same way?

12

———

Simon

A day passed after the Great Musubi Moment, and then another day, and Simon was beginning to wonder if he'd imagined the spark between him and Leilani. But then his mind would play things over again and no, there was no way he could imagine something like that.

But Leilani went right on with working like nothing was the matter, and his brothers continued moving on with all their projects, once again leaving Simon by the wayside.

On the positive side, they did tend to include him in more of their plans, leaving him with fewer days of just sitting around trying to plan for a future that he had no ideas for. And he was pretty sure he hadn't seen his mom so happy in years. Her and Auntie Kini were two peas in a pod, often spending most of their day together. In fact, the only time he really saw them apart was if Mom was attending a business dinner with Dad or if Auntie Kini was at physical therapy.

But Simon was growing more restless by the day. He liked having Leilani around. In fact, he wouldn't mind her staying forever, but he hated that there was a trio of men out there, looking to hurt her. He wished she'd open up to him, open up to any of them and tell them what happened, but as far as he knew, Leilani didn't care to discuss it.

"Hey, Auntie Kini didn't happen to tell you anything about those men, did she?" he asked as he and his mom took a walk around her garden. She'd expanded on it in the years that he'd been gone, and it really was amazingly lush and full of life. Teddy was center, pruning tomatoes—she was the only one Mom trusted to do so—while Frenchie was dutifully rooting around the cucumbers for the last that would be produced before summer grew too scalding for even them.

"Simon, are you trying to get me to spill secrets?"

"No, not secrets. Just wondering if you knew."

"Wouldn't that be a violation of girl code if I told you what my BFF said to me in confidence?"

Simon affixed his mom with a confused look. "Who taught you that and why are you choosing to use it?"

"Francesca, of course. Are you saying that I'm not hip with the kids, Simon?"

"I mean, you did have it replaced, so I suppose your hip is only a teenager."

She huffed and joshed his arm. "Smart aleck. You're lucky you're my son and I like you so much."

"Yeah, I am."

His mom smiled and rested her head against his arm. "No, she didn't tell me anything, by the way. I wish either of them would open up, but Auntie Kini is very firmly in the camp of it being Leilani's story to tell and no one else's."

"I really wish she trusted us enough to say something."

"Me too, my darling, me too. But until she is ready, we will be here, patiently waiting."

Simon nodded his head, trying to enjoy the moment as they walked around the beautiful space that his mom had spent so much time making. Perhaps he could help her with the harvest and the planting of it next year.

If he was still around.

As his mom stopped to refill her hummingbird feeder, Simon checked his phone. He was just beginning to thumb through his emails when his phone rang. In a rare moment of serendipity, he realized that it was the private investigator that he and his mom had decided to hire to track down the trio since the cops weren't making any headway.

"Mr. Simon Miller?" the voice on the other end asked. It was just about exactly as he would imagine the man sounding, all gruff and raspy.

"Yes, this is he. Detective Speidle?"

"None other. I have some interesting developments. I'd like to meet with you to discuss things."

"Is that necessary? Do PIs usually do house calls?"

"No, not usually. But there's... there's a lot here that I didn't expect to find, and I think showing you all the documentation in person will be easier than scanning it and explaining each document via email."

Simon's stomach dropped. There was *a lot* of documentation? That couldn't be good. But also, it had to mean that he had a strong trail, right?

"How soon can you get here?"

"Let me GPS you... Alright, it's quite a drive. I can get there in about three hours, give or take."

"I'll be here. Oh, and let's meet at the front so I can take you to our mechanic's area. We don't have anything being worked on right now, so we'll be able to spread things out and talk in private."

"Sounds good, Mr. Miller. I'll see you then."

He hung up. Although Simon was able to finish his walk with his mom, he was practically vibrating with anticipation. Finally, *finally*, they were getting somewhere with Leilani's case.

Those three hours were some of the most painful ones that he had been through in a long while, and when the PI finally pulled up in a black jeep, he was all too anxious to hop in and direct him to the garage.

The PI didn't say much during the drive, just went over some basics about the services he used to find his information and how everything was on the up and up. Simon nodded along eagerly and all but vaulted himself out of the car once they arrived at the garage.

It was sweltering inside since no one was around to use it, so Simon turned the AC on full blast while the PI continued to discuss the banal stuff outside. By the time he got the man over to one of the mechanic's tables, he was beside himself wanting to know *what* the man had learned.

"So, there's something you're not telling me," the man said finally.

"Hmmm?" Simon asked, his eyebrows going up to his hairline.

"Almost all of this paperwork is related to a single woman that one of these men has been stalking and harassing for years. All three have a couple of minor incidents, traffic tickets, loitering, misdemeanor stuff, but everything big is related to this woman." The PI paused for emphasis. "A woman that your company just happened to hire this summer."

"...Leilani," Simon said.

"Good, so you do know her. One Leilani Kamea Cunningham. Age twenty-three. She was born in Honolulu, where she lived with her mother and father and four other siblings. According to what I could dig up, her father died when she was seventeen, which is when she transitioned from a part-time job at a local ice cream shop to work nearly full time in the evenings as a waitress."

Simon could only blink as his brain absorbed the information. Leilani's father was dead? She'd been working even before she was seventeen? She had *four* other siblings? He ate up the crumbs like they were some kind of gourmet food while the back of his mind was screaming questions about what *everything big* could possibly mean.

"After reading all these police reports and restraining orders, interviews and the like, I've put together a timeline." The man opened the messenger bag and was suddenly laying out several manila folders, each one meticulously organized with a series of letters and colors.

"Don't try to figure out my labeling system," the PI said gruffly. "It's just what works for me. Anyway, let's start with this one."

He opened the farthest and thinnest folder, which contained what seemed to be some sort of protective order by the label at the top.

"Mind you, these aren't in chronological order. This is the file where mostly I organize them in order of the information given. So this report details how they met, ergo, I put it first. You can see here that they met when he was a customer at her restaurant and asked her out. She was seventeen and he was twenty, and according to her he seemed both sweet and mature."

Simon paled as those words wrapped around him. "He who?"

"Oh, did I not mention that earlier? Kai Inthavong. Local gang member." The PI cleared his throat. "Now, something important to know—it helped me understand this case better—is that gangs in Hawaii are different than gangs here. Mostly graffiti, theft and drug-related activity. Gun violence or murder is *very* rare in Hawaii. I guess it's an island thing? Hard to do terrible things in such a small place without hurting someone you love. Anyway, this will become important later, so keep that in the back of your mind."

Simon nodded, but his brain was already putting together the pieces. Kai was the one Leilani was scared of. Kai had asked Leilani out at her work, just like Simon had. No wonder she turned him down. But had he scared her when he'd done that? He hadn't meant to, but did that even matter?

"Anyway, they go on a few dates and, although it doesn't say why here, Leilani eventually decided to call it off. As you can guess, Mr. Kai didn't take it well. If you turn over the stapled report, the next thick chunk of papers is her call and text logs."

Simon woodenly did as he directed, and sure enough there was an intimidatingly thick stack of papers with lines of info sorted into gray and white tabs.

"As you can see from the first five pages, he called her almost a thousand times over two weeks. That's basically seventy-two times a day, three every hour. He called at all times of the night, and we think he also called from random numbers, but those couldn't be verified. And I wish I could say all he did was call, but on the next page, you will literally see the thousands upon thousands of texts he sent before Miss Cunningham changed her number.

Simon's stomach was clenching, and he felt sweat breaking out along his brow despite the AC. It was so much worse than he thought. A tale of horror was unrolling in front of his eyes, painting a vivid picture. He wanted to turn it off, to shut his lids and say that he'd heard enough, but if Leilani had lived through it, the least he could do was listen.

Or read, as was the case.

Where are U?

Come on, babe, I miss U

Ur confused. It's OK. Ur still a baby. Imma take care of U

Yo, tell ur cuz if he want me 2 buss him up, keep runnin his mouth!

Ur being a child. ANSWER THE PHONE

Wat's the matter, Leilei? U don't miss my kisses? Missed the way I touched you? Ain't nobody gonna love u cept me.

FATTIE.

NO ONE WILL EVER LOVE U. UR DISGUSTING. UR LUCKY I EVEN LOOKED UR WAY.

How u gonna turn down someı like me? I make money on money, I have my own place. A car. I'm strong enough 2 guide you, help you with that temper. I am the best ur ever going to get, but you leave me on the street like trash? Insanity.

I would take care of U like you deserve. Treat u like a Queen. Let me worship u, make u feel good. Don't I make u feel good?

STOP THIS LOLO ACT AND CALL ME.

I swear Imma smack u in the head until you start acting right. RESPECT ME.

Baby, baby, ur so beautiful. I need u. NEED. I can't breathe w/o U

OH SO NOW U SEND UR CUZINS TO TALK STINK WIT MY CREW??? U MUST BE LOLO. U IN FOR A WORLD OF HURT!

I kno where u live, Leilei, why make it like this?

I don't' want to hurt u, I don't want seeing u cry. Let's make this better, ok? <3

SIMON ANGRILY PUSHED the papers away, not even through the second page. He was going to be sick outright now.

What he read was worse than repugnant. Worse than disgusting. It was evil, pure and simple, spelled out in a myriad of chat bubbles.

And there were apparently *thousands* of them. *Thousands!* He didn't understand how it was possible, but his hands curled at his sides, his whole body shaking with the thought that the man responsible for all the mess he'd read had been in his home.

"After she changed her number, things escalated. After the text packet, you can see the report where three of their house windows were smashed in. Then Mrs. Cunningham's car tires were slashed. All minor stuff until, apparently, Kai cornered two of her siblings on their walk home from school and threatened them.

"This is where that gang factoid comes in. Kai was the second in his gang, well-trusted and a right-hand man to their leader. But when it came back to his crew what he was doing to the Cunninghams, they outright kicked him."

"Kicked him?"

"Fully removed him. And none of the other local gangs would take him either. See, everyone tends to know everyone on the islands, especially in the native communities, so Leilani either had a cousin or a family friend or even some of the young ones she used to babysit in every group in the neighborhood.

"This apparently wasn't a good lesson, however, because Kai became feral. A loose cannon. You can flip through reports to see some of the instances of what he did. Showing up at her work. Grabbing her hair but then letting go, trying to break into her house, watching her, hounding her for her new number. It all culminated in him trying to set fire to her family home, and that was when the very first restraining order was placed. This is actually the first document ever filed with the police, but I placed it here because it's only really dealing with the work incident and the house fire."

Simon's hand kept up, but his mind wasn't reading anymore. He was horrified, through and through. Kai had tried to burn down Leilani's house? Threatened her younger siblings? How was he not in *jail!?*

"It appears he kept to this restraining order for almost a year, but only just. Apparently, he would stand the appropriate three hundred feet away and just watch her. He'd make sure he was visible, sitting in a lawn chair on top of cars, or the hill on the beach. He was always beyond the allotted distance, though. And if they did call the cops, he'd say he was bird watching with his binoculars."

"And that went on for a year?"

"Yes. But then it seems he started to escalate again when Miss Cunningham turned nineteen. It doesn't say if there's a specific event that triggered it, but he began to send her things. Some vile, some inappropriate. You can see pictures of each item if you keep going."

The horror continued, one right after the other. By the time Simon was through that stack, he was numb.

"Please tell me that's it. That has to be it."

"'Fraid not. But I'll skip to the end. This whole situation seemed to culminate with Miss Cunningham going to the movies with one of her cousins who was visiting from Japan. I'm not sure if this is a blood cousin or a family friend given that the locals of Hawaii seem to use the terms interchangeably, but in this instance it doesn't matter.

"The point is, Kai saw Leilani with a male he didn't recognize, misinterpreted it as a date, and when they came out, he and his two lackeys jumped the pair."

"Jumped."

"Yeah, as in—"

"I know what it means. But they... they beat up the both of them?"

"Yes. The cousin definitely had it worse, and it delayed his return home to Japan, but Miss Cunningham didn't escape their wrath. Next are some of the pictures of her injuries."

Simon stared down at the last piece of paper covering up what the detective was talking about, his last shield against seeing something that he very much didn't want to see. But like watching a car wreck in slow motion, his hand lifted, and he turned that page just like all the rest of them.

And there was Leilani's face, lip split, one brow swollen, dark bruises peppering her face. It was too much. She looked so haunted, so scared. The next thing Simon knew, he was pushing away from the table and speed walking to the minifridge, where he grabbed a water bottle and chugged it in the hoped that it would stop him from losing his lunch.

"It's not the worst I've seen, and there's no permanent damage, but it's not pretty."

"I don't understand," Simon rasped when he could talk without puking. "Why isn't he in *jail*? Why is he here?"

There was no doubt in his mind that Kai should be locked up and the key melted down until there was nothing left. The cruelty in which he stalked Leilani, terrorized her... Simon couldn't even imagine.

And oh my goodness, he'd done the same thing. Sure, he hadn't meant it maliciously, but for four days after Kai had showed up, Simon had made sure he'd watched her from a distance.

Oh *no*.

"The details aren't entirely clear, but he was only charged with a misdemeanor assault with a sentence of one year which he pled guilty to. He did get out two months early on good behavior. If I had to guess, it was definitely a plea deal that the prosecution worked out because they weren't confident in Miss Cunningham's case."

That was enough to shock Simon back into the moment. "Not confident? Why?"

"You don't want me to actually answer that."

Simon's temper flared. He was just so angry at *all* of it. How a man dared to do that to Leilani, how a human could hurt another human so. How the justice system had clearly failed her when she'd tried to go through all the steps.

"No, I do. Please."

The PI was quiet. "It's just going to make you angry."

"I'm already angry."

"In my professional opinion—"

"*Tell. Me.*"

"Alright." The PI drew a breath. "People deserve to be judged by a jury of their peers, but a lot of times in Hawaii, the natives get excused from jury duty. They can't afford to miss that much work, even if their time is compensated for, while the rich, white foreigners that come over and speculatively buy up properties and drive up prices have all the time in the world. Chances were, Leilani would be looking at a full jury of people who aren't all that familiar with island life *while* having a lot of Eurocentric ideals."

"I can see why that might matter if Kai was white and she wasn't, but they're both clearly brown," Simon said carefully, trying to push his anger down enough so that he could understand what the detective was saying.

"Yes, they are. I'm going to stop trying to put this delicately. Miss Cunningham is plus-sized, tall and broad, not exactly a pale, willowy maiden that needs protecting. Meanwhile, Kai is incredibly fit, a very good-looking dude by European standards. Convincing a group of people with mainlander senses of beauty and goodness that an incredibly attractive man was chasing after a fat, dark-skinned woman was difficult enough.

"When you add in that Kai had photos of Leilani in… compromising positions, well that muddied the water further."

If possible, that was the worst thing Simon could have heard in that moment. "What do you mean?"

"You know exactly what I mean, and I don't think it's necessary to go into it. Point being, they knew there was a large chance they would lose, so they went with the shorter sentence. When word got out that Kai was going to be released, Mrs. Cunningham sent her daughter to live in the States. She's been here for about three years, most of that time living with her relative, a Mrs. Kilikina ʻŌpūnui, who is her Great Aunt on her maternal side."

Auntie Kini. Of course.

"How did he find her?"

"It seems that Miss Cunningham has been incredibly good about her social media. Only pictures featuring plants, or animals, no details, or very close pictures of her face, or even outfits of the day. It's impressively meticulous, actually, but then there was a single tagged photo."

He slid over another picture and Simon recognized Nova, Frenchie, and Leilani all together by the pond and taking a selfie.

"It's from a different account, one run by Nova Clarke, but it tags your ranch in it. That's how they must have found out."

That was it.

That was all Kai had needed to run in and ruin Leilani's life again. Just a single photo.

"So what do we do?" Simon asked, feeling defeated. And also... like he'd failed? He wanted to protect Leilani, to see her smile and happy and content, but so much had already happened before he even knew her. How was he supposed to fix that? How could he protect her from someone who the law seemed to let do what he wanted?

"This is going to sound callous, but I don't think we should pursue the Leilani angle at all. Instead, we should go for destruction of property and assault on your two brothers and the fiancée. Courts are much more likely to go after someone who damages things for the rich than care about a poor brown woman's stalker, to put it frankly. Plus, I'm sure your family pays quite a lot for a whole team of lawyers."

"We do."

"Good. Now, I've been looking into their connections, trying to find patterns, but these guys are slippery. I'm fairly sure they won't leave without Leilani, but I can't help but feel like we've got a clock over their heads. The cops aren't dedicating much time to this, so I suggest your family use their influence to lean in. Put the pressure on."

Simon nodded, but there, in the very back of his mind, an idea started to come to him. "What if... what if we could do something to lure them out into the open?"

"If you have a way to do that, I'd be mighty keen to hear it."

13

———————

Leilani

*L*eilani was surprised by the knock on her room door. It was midweek and right in that nebulous time after supper, but before bed, where everyone sort of broke off to do their own thing. She'd been resting, reading a book about gardening that Teddy swore by, and almost dropped it.

Heading over, she was surprised to open it and see Simon standing there, looking every bit the handsome rancher that she barely knew.

"Do you trust me enough to try something completely crazy if it means getting rid of Kai once and for all?"

Her stomach dropped, hitting the ground somewhere far below her feet.

"How do you know about Kai?" Sure, she'd mentioned his name once in passing, but it wasn't something that seemed important enough for Simon to remember.

"I'm sorry, I didn't mean to pry into your history, but our family's PI did some digging and found...well, a lot."

Time did that awful slowing down thing again as Leilani's mind caught up. He knew? He knew about how naïve she'd been? How she'd ran away and given up hope on justice? She *hated* that. She didn't want to be the victim. Poor, little airheaded Leilani who got caught up with an older man. She should have—

Her heart suddenly thumped. Had Simon seen the pictures?

Oh no. No, no, *no*. She couldn't look him in the eye if he—

"I didn't mean to violate your privacy, but I have a plan. It's insane. It's dangerous. But I think it'll work since it's clear that the cops aren't taking this seriously."

Somehow his words made it to her brain, and she swallowed thickly. It didn't sound like he was judging her. Or thinking poorly of her.

"...a plan?"

He nodded, looking eager in a way that she didn't understand. Why wasn't he blaming her? Or dismissing the whole experience? Why wasn't he telling her it was her fault for getting involved with a gang member?

"Yeah, a plan."

She hadn't told many people about what happened mostly because she didn't like to think about it. Wiping out the three years between seventeen and twenty was easier than facing the specter that haunted her thoughts.

"What is it?"

"Well," he said, looking like he was debating telling her at all. But there was a fire in him. The type of fire that had long since gone out in Leilani. "How do you feel about your acting skills?"

"Are you sure this is enough?" she asked over the music playing from her phone, a smile pasted over her face as she shoved her bag into the back of Simon's truck.

"Oh yeah," he said, projecting over the music too. "We're only camping for a couple of days. We don't need to over-supply."

"Alright, if you say so. I'm not exactly an expert at this."

Suddenly Simon was right next to her, and he gave her a wink that made her heart beat faster than it should have. "Don't worry. I'll teach you."

Man, she'd always thought she was a pretty good actor, but Simon made her feel like a novice. She swallowed hard, nodding, then hopped into his truck.

If he noticed her odd reaction, he didn't say. He merely grinned and sauntered around the truck before getting in the driver's seat and cranking up the music.

They drove out of the front of the estate and down the road going the speed limit, making a real spectacle of themselves. It was funny how loud they were being, how opposite of their usual natures, but that was the whole point of it.

It took them about an hour and a half to reach their mark rather than the hour fifteen that they had been shooting for, but hopefully that wouldn't throw anything off. Leilani swallowed thickly, then got out of the truck.

The trail was beautiful, trees thick and forming natural groves where it looked like people camped plenty of times. The truck was pulled onto a grassy area with a sunbeam coming down onto it, and she could hear rushing water not far away.

Gosh, she missed the clear, shining water of home. Was

there anywhere that could match the beauty of the ocean that touched her islands? She didn't think so.

"Are you sure this is going to work?" she whispered to Simon, drawing up close to him so that, to anyone watching, it just looked like an intimate moment between a couple.

"I'm pretty sure they're watching the comings and goings of the house, trying to catch you when you leave a shift."

"How could you possibly know that?"

"Well, I don't *know* it, but it's something I did once when I was trying to catch a pickpocket that stole all my IDs when I was abroad. Well, something similar at least."

That was something she wanted to hear about, but maybe another day.

Instead they went about loudly setting up their camp. While Leilani kept her outer demeanor fun and excited, inside she was both terrified and incredibly curious. It was like Simon was opening up right in front of her, but she couldn't figure out what was real and what was an act.

Did he want to catch Kai and his friends because of all the damage they had done to Simon's house, or was it something more? It seemed impossible that the already generous man wanted to catch these guys for *her*, but some back part of her mind hoped that was the case.

But that was silly. She didn't need a man to save her. A man was exactly what ruined her life in the first place.

...yet Simon felt different.

And maybe that's why it was so easy to pretend to be a couple. She could still remember Kai's virulent reaction when he thought she'd dared to go on a date with someone. It wasn't a date, of course, just a meeting with her cousin who she missed terribly since he'd moved to Japan when he was eleven, but Kai wouldn't listen to her. She could still hear her own voice screaming, her pleading with him to stop hitting her. And she could hear his fist connecting with her cheek too.

The weird thing was, in that moment when he'd actually struck her, she'd felt relief. Finally she had *real*, palpable damage that was going to get him locked away. Sure, he was beating her up good, knocking aside her attempts to block or hit back, but it had been her key to freedom. She'd worn those bruises proudly into the police station and pressed assault charges with plenty of photographic evidence to back things up.

But then that hadn't worked either. It had bought her time, but only ten short months.

Part of her was sure that Simon's plan wouldn't work either and that she was doomed to be stalked, hunted for the rest of her life. Always running, always trying to carve out a few years of safety before having to run again. But another part of her, the part that always tried to cling to what was good in life, wanted to believe that maybe, just maybe, things would work out.

Simon's hand alighted on the small of her back sent a thrill of excitement through her that wasn't fake at all. When was the last time she had let anyone touch her? Even pretending to be a couple was reminding her of everything she'd been missing out on. Everything she was too exhausted or scared to dream of.

If Kai was gone, what would she do? Would she finally *date*? It was hard to say. So many of her firsts, the precious milestones of falling in love, had been stolen by someone truly evil. Would she ever be able to move past that?

She supposed she would find out. She knew from experience that the close contact would rile Kai up if he was watching. After all, according to him, he still owned her.

"Hey there, handsome," she said, turning to Simon as if she

was going to press herself to his front. Not quite touching, but almost there, their bodies able to sense the close proximity, but still the thrill of just *barely* being denied.

She would be lying if she said it wasn't *nice*. Because it was. Looking up into Simon's eyes, it was easy to imagine a world without Kai. A world where she got to be a normal teenager. A normal young adult. Where she got to go to college and didn't have to live in exile from her home.

It was easy to imagine an untraumatized Leilani coming home from a long day of work, kissing Simon's cheek, then going to soak her feet in the tub while he brought up snacks. It was easy to envision going on dates. Seeing a movie. Holding hands and walking in public while they fell bit by bit in love with each other.

But just as easily as that impossible daydream came, it popped just as quickly at the sound of a particularly loud branch snapping behind them. She jerked, whirling around, and at the same time Simon stepped around her so that he was between her and where the sound had come from.

Sure enough, three figures emerged from the woods. It was like not a single day had passed, and suddenly Leilani was that same nineteen-year-old watching the trio emerge from the parking lot in front of the cinema. Terrified out of her mind and knowing that something terrible was coming.

"You?" Simon said, sounding shocked.

Leilani glanced from him to the specters of her past, wondering how he recognized them.

"Hey cuz. Thanks for the advice before. Your ranch really was a good distance away still. Can't bring a car from the islands, you know?"

"You tricked me."

"You know him?" Leilani asked. She thought that Simon

had missed the fight after she'd warned Mrs. Miller about what was going on.

"We met," Simon ground out. "Once."

But it had been a mistake to speak, because she could feel when her hunter's eyes landed right on her.

"Leilani," Kai said, stepping forward, his grin just as wide and broad as she remembered.

Goodness, it was like he hadn't even aged a day. His hair was still thick and healthy, pulled back into that ponytail that she used to think was so stylish, so masculine. It was common in her culture for warriors and strong men to be equated with long, voluminous hair. She'd never understood why it was the opposite on the mainland, but surely, even most *haoles* could see the beauty and power in Kai's features.

Except she knew those looks were just a mask for an ugly, disgusting monster that laid underneath. A monster who hurt her, but more importantly, hurt her family. She wanted to rip him limb from limb, and yet she was ashamed that all she'd been able to do so far was run.

"I'm giving you a warning," Simon said, his voice icier than Leilani had ever heard it. Almost dangerous. It was bizarre considering the man had only been either charming, neutral, or painfully kind with her. Maybe all those muscles of his and that chiseled jawline weren't just for decoration.

"I wasn't talking to you, cuz. This is between me and my lady."

It was tempting to just cower behind Simon. To let his strong voice and broad frame protect her from her worst nightmare. But some part of her wouldn't allow that. It was that same spark that always got her into trouble, but she was never quite able to snuff out.

"I'm not your lady, Kai."

The man's face didn't even twitch. "Girls always playing hard to get, you know?"

"She's not a girl," Simon countered. "She's a woman, and I believe this woman would like it if you left."

Philandro stepped up, lips pulled back in a snarl. Leilani recognized him too. He'd been a mean kid, kicking dogs and terrorizing cats and geckos. She'd never liked him, and at the moment, she found she liked him even less.

"Kai, why are we wasti—"

But their leader just held up a single finger to silence him.

"Look, I know when I was younger, I made things messy. I have a lot to apologize for."

It was almost like a siren's song, all honey and oil, his big, green eyes watering and his beautiful lips pulled back in what looked like a sincere apology. But Leilani knew better. She'd been bitten by that shark before, when she was just a naïve teenager and he'd pinned her down in the back seat of his car and yanked a kiss from her mouth while she objected.

That was when she'd decided to break it off with him. It was just a kiss, but it was her first one, and he'd taken it from her when she wasn't ready. But then he'd pleaded with her, begged, said he misinterpreted her body language, and then for some crazy reason, she'd decided to give him another chance.

But the next time they'd been alone together, he'd pressured her to kiss him again. And if there was a single thing that she had learned, it was that if Kai wanted something, he got it.

Kai always got what he wanted, just not in a respectable way.

"But I've grown, baby. I'm better than ever. I've been to therapy, and I've got my anger in check." He took a step forward, and even though he was taller than her, he still managed to look up at her through his lashes. Kai always had lovely lashes... she vaguely remembered being jealous of them when she first met him. "I miss you, baby. I ain't never met anybody as pretty or as smart as you. Let's go home, okay? I know your family misses you. Don't you miss home? You belong in Hawaii."

Of course, she missed home. But it wasn't home he was offering. Just a cage in a tropical setting.

"I'm not interested, Kai. I don't want to date you, and I'm not yours."

She assumed it was her ancestors who gave her the strength to hold her voice steady, because she felt like she might shake apart at any moment.

"You heard her, friend. She isn't interested."

Another step forward and Leilani could see Kai's musculature tensing. Both the men in front of her were radiating strength and challenge. "Look, I'm being kind here because you gave me and my friends directions. Clear out, and none of this has to be messy. This is a family matter."

"I gave you directions and then you proceeded to *fight* my family. I don't see why I shouldn't lay you out right here and now."

No, no, he shouldn't antagonize them. It was so easy to have bravado, but it was going to be three against two, and both Kai and Philando had trained at the same MMA gym. They were fast and smart and *good* at what they did.

"Hey, we had no intention of doing anything. Your brother and his lady came in swinging."

"Yeah, because you were destroying my mom's kitchen!"

"Kitchen? And here we thought it was some sort of plantation-themed small restaurant." Kai and his friends chuckled, making Leilani's blood run cold. "These the kind of folks you running with, girl? Never thought that you were about the dollar."

"I'm not," she countered, licking her lips. She needed to stall. Buy time. That was the whole point of it, right? To draw Kai and his friends out into the open long enough so that law enforcement could snatch them up. That was why there was a camera set up on Simon's dash that was livestreaming to several law enforcement officers hidden in their non-marked cars nearby. Apparently that family PI of theirs had some favors to call in. "They gave me a good job. Got tired of being a waitress."

"Baby, you know I said you should never have to work a day in your life. Come on, let me take care of you so you can do whatever your heart wants."

"What my heart wants is for you to leave me alone."

That perfect, beautiful, apologetic expression of his started to crack, the tears in the corners of his eyes beginning to dry. "Why do you always have to be difficult?"

"Difficult?" Leilani shot back before she could think better of it. "Is that what you call stalking me? Threatening me? Scaring my little brothers and sisters? You made me move to the *mainland*, Kai. That's literally a different continent, practically a different world to get away from *you*."

"That's about as clear a no as you can get," Simon said. "Last chance. You clear out, you finally get over this, and you get to walk. But you stay here, and you're finally going to pay the consequences of your actions."

"Oh yeah?" Kai asked. "And who's gonna make me pay then? You?"

Simon let out such a dry chuckle that it was practically dust. "Hardly. You've got..." He looked down at his watch. "...about two minutes to make the smart choice, or the foolish one."

"You talk a big game, *haole*." Kai nodded to his two lackeys who began to spread apart. Her hand carefully went to the fire poker that she had set aside just moments earlier, preparing for anything.

And for some reason, Leilani was suddenly reminded of the old spaghetti westerns she used to watch with her mom. It was a standoff, alright, three versus two, all of them waiting for someone to draw and get the party started.

Of course, that never happened, because sirens sounded all around them, flashing lights flickering through the thick trees.

"What's goin' on here?" Kai asked, taking a step back and looking behind him.

"Ah, looks like your time is up. This is the end of the road, Kai. You're never going to bother Leilani again."

Leilani didn't believe in revenge, or taking joy in the pain of others, but the look of shock that crossed Kai's features as he realized that he'd been set up was something she would treasure for quite a while.

"You betrayed me, Leilei?"

"My name is *Leilani Kamea Cunningham*," she seethed, tension radiating through her body. "But you're not going to get a chance to call me that, because I'm never going to see you again."

There was the sound of people moving through the trees, then multiple things were happening at the once.

There was a flash in Kai's hand, glittering in the light. A knife. Simon must have seen it too, because suddenly he was rushing forward, colliding with the man in an effort to stop him in the middle of his charge at Leilani.

Uniformed men were crashing through the foliage all around them. It was loud, there was shouting, the two other men put their hands up and got down on their knees in surrender.

Kai and Simon were somehow on the ground. Leilani didn't know if Simon had tackled him or if her stalker had taken him down. She couldn't tell who was winning, who was losing. Her brain was awash with so much information at once, and she'd never been much of a fighter. Sure, she'd brawled, she knew the peripherals of street fighting, but not the smooth, practiced techniques that the men in front of her used.

Officers rushed forward and grabbed at Kai, who resisted them, yanking him away from Simon. The man who protected her without a second thought. There was more white noise in her head as Kai screamed and thrashed, threatening her in every way in the book. Calling her some of the worst names a woman can be called. Then, the police officer started reading him his rights, as were others to his two friends.

But the maelstrom died back ever so slightly when Simon shakily made his way to his feet. She knew that she was high on adrenaline and terror, but watching him rise up, the afternoon sun glowing behind him and the breeze gently tugging at his clothes and hair, she couldn't help but think he looked every bit the image of a hero.

Her own, personal hero.

She couldn't describe the feelings churning within her. She was incredulous that their plan had worked. Relieved that it had. She was still terrified by everything that had unfolded. Still shaking from defying Kai right to his face. She'd stared her monster down and—

Why was there a red spot on Simon's shirt!

She lurched forward; hands outstretched. "Are you alright?" She heard herself ask desperately. If Simon had gotten hurt defending her... if he... if...

"Of course." He gave her a curious glance before his eyes followed her horrified stare. The red spot was growing, seeping into the light color of his shirt with speed. "Oh. When did that happen?" he asked, his face growing pale. He wavered once and Leilani rushed to his side, catching his strong frame against her soft one.

"It's okay," she said, helping him sit down. "I got you. You took care of me, now I got you, okay?" He nodded dully, looking confused about the whole situation, but Leilani just took a deep breath and let out the loudest shout she could. *"I need a paramedic!"*

14

Simon

*S*imon had never had stitches before and, to be perfectly honest, he wasn't the biggest fan of them. They were a bit itchy and a lot pully, and none of his pain meds had even worn off yet. But still, as his brother Solomon came to pick him up, he couldn't help but feel perhaps somewhat like a badass.

He wished that Leilani could have stayed with him. His thoughts were hazy after he realized that Kai's knife had managed to get one small but effective slash in him, but he remembered her comforting words, her soft hands, the way her gray eyes looked at him with such attention that it made him feel like he was the center of the whole world and everything would be alright.

The wound hadn't been too bad. Nowhere near anything vital, but the center of it, just above his hip bone, had gone to just about a quarter of an inch depth, hence the stitches. He was going to have a scar, but it was so tiny that he wouldn't even be able to brag about it.

Oh well. He was just glad that it wasn't serious.

And that Leilani was safe.

She was giving her statement to the cops. Whisked away from Simon when he'd been loaded into an ambulance. He didn't like that he couldn't see her, that she was surrounded by police officers that she didn't trust or know, but Sal had texted him that he and Silas were both with her.

Still, he wanted to see her. He wanted to check if she was alright and also see what it was like to witness a woman be free after being hunted for so long. Had it even hit her yet? He had no idea. He couldn't even imagine how she felt, but he hoped it was wonderful. Truly wonderful.

"You seem like you're remarkably happy for a guy who just got stabbed," Solomon remarked as they drove along, city fading to the highway that led to their estate.

"Not stabbed, slashed. There's a difference," Simon replied with a grin. Yeah, they definitely loaded him up on maybe a bit too much medication. He wasn't out of it, but the whole situation seemed a lot more happy and humorous than it probably should have. "If it was a stabbing, it'd be much more serious. You know, cause kidneys and stuff."

"Ah yes, and stuff. How could I have forgotten."

Simon laughed again. His brother was funny. Why had he never thought about Solomon being funny?

"You know, I realize you might not be entirely upstairs right now, but I wanted to remind you that my wedding *is* coming up in a month and you still haven't RSVP'd. I sent you a couple emails, but I didn't get a reply, and we usually keep missing each other at the house."

"I didn't think I needed to RSVP, brother. *Of course*, I'm going to be there. Like I would miss the first wedding of our generation. Although, you know, I really thought it was going to be Samuel and that Marilyn Monroe of his first."

"I realize you might be the slightest bit inebriated right now, but that's a fairly accurate depiction."

"Just more physically fit." Simon laughed. "How do I suddenly know so many women with biceps that look like they could bench press more than me? Missy, Monroe-lady, Teddy, Elizabeth."

"You're getting sidetracked, but yeah." He heard Solomon's soft laugh from beside him and shot his brother a grin.

It was just like old times, one of his elder brothers driving him to sports or school or even just the mall while they talked about things that mattered to them. How had they gotten away from that? Simon *liked* all those rides.

"I'm more interested in if you were bringing a guest. You know, like maybe a certain island girl who you've been—"

"Tell me, how is it that all of you are so far up in my business?" Simon countered before he could finish. "I didn't do that to any of *you*."

"You weren't around, Simon."

Oh.

That was right.

He'd been at college. Exploring. Experiencing life outside of the ranch. Hiding? Maybe? Why did so many of his motivations seem like they were just excuses for getting away from his family and everything that was expected of him?

Whew, that was a thought.

"Well, I haven't even asked Leilani, so that's probably a solid no."

"Look, it's fine if you want to ride solo. But if you want to ask

Leilani, you should. It's not every day a person saves someone from their violent stalker."

"I didn't *save* her," Simon argued, and he could hear the petulance in his own voice. "Leilani saved herself all on her own, I just gave her the tools. Cause, ya know, we've got a lot of tools."

"That we do, Simon, that we do."

The conversation drifted from there and Simon wasn't sure if he quite followed it, but before he knew it, they were back home.

Suddenly his mom was right there. To his mind, it was like she teleported beside him, arms flung open wide to hug him, but she was stopped short by Leilani's gentle hand on her shoulder.

"Be careful, Mrs. Miller."

"Oh, that's right. What was I thinking!" His mom looked up at him, tears in the corner of her eyes.

All Simon could think about was how much he loved his mom and how he felt like he had somewhat let her down. He couldn't say how, but it was a feeling that punched his gut.

"Hey, Momma," he said with a sleepy grin. "You can hug me. Just be gentle and avoid my right side."

Mrs. Miller nodded tearfully and oh-so-gently hugged him. Maybe it was strange for a twenty-four-year-old man to feel so protected in his mom's arms, but it really did center him. He kinda got, in a hazy way, why his family could be content with their worlds not extending that far outside of Dallas. There was just so much *there*.

"My baby, my crazy baby. I'm so glad you're here. You're safe."

"I am," Simon confirmed with a nod before his gaze went to Leilani.

She was watching, an expression on her face that he'd never seen before. She almost looked... peaceful? Maybe that wasn't the right word for it. There was happiness and sheepishness, and also plenty of worry etched into her features. But also... a lightness to her? Maybe that was a better way to say it. He didn't know. He definitely needed that pain medication out of his system so his words would come back.

He liked words.

"Why don't we get you in and up to bed. I'll bring you something to drink and some comfort food, how about that?"

Food? Food sounded *amazing*. Why hadn't Simon thought about food? He'd been too wound up to eat before their fake camping trip, and he realized it had been hours and hours since he'd last eaten. Food was *great*.

"Yeah, Mom. That sounds nice."

Was his accent thicker or were his ears thicker? Wait, ears didn't get thick. Whatever. He just wanted to lay down and let his body do its thing until his mind was back to normal.

"I can take him upstairs," Leilani said softly. "If you want to finish up with his food and things."

Mom nodded, finally releasing him. "That sounds like a plan, honey. Take care of my boy."

"Don't worry, I will." She gave a nod to Solomon, who flashed a smile before hopping back into his truck to pull it around to the back. Leilani then offered her hand to Simon.

Simon stared at her palm, knowing how soft it was. How cool it had felt before against his fevered skin. For some reason, he wasn't quite sure if he would take it. If he was crossing a boundary he wasn't supposed to.

Because he wanted to grip her hand. He wanted to feel her skin against his, learn everything about her and always be in her orbit. But he was her boss and she was scared and...

"It's okay, Simon. Let me take you upstairs."

Oh, he had permission. Okay, that was good.

His hand slid into hers and it seemed to fit just right, like they were made for each other. That was a silly thing to think, and yet he thought it anyway.

'Cause the truth was, he knew from the moment that he'd first interacted with her in that diner that there was something special about Leilani. She was like another half that he hadn't known he was missing. She was light and wit and vibrance, and something about her made him feel more centered.

Too bad she clearly didn't feel the same way.

It was kind of a cruel joke, really. To show him someone he realized he desperately needed... someone who had no need for him. Maybe it was a punishment for... he didn't really know what it could be for, actually.

He wasn't entirely with it, trusting Leilani to guide him, but she stopped suddenly, and Simon didn't quite get the memo, bumping against her back. She didn't move, however, able to support his somewhat drunken weight, and Simon just reveled in the soft press of her against him.

She felt so *nice*. Did she know she felt nice? Probably. Leilani knew a lot of stuff. Simon wished he could wrap his arms around her and hold her like that forever. Warm and good and wonderful against him, a refuge in the storm.

It was only after several long moments that he realized someone was talking tersely to her.

"—my son has been injured because of the trouble you brought here! What did I say? I know the kind of trouble that follows people like you, and I knew you were going to pull us into it."

Oh.

It was his dad. Great.

But Leilani's voice was the smoothest steel as she answered. "Your son was injured apprehending the men who ransacked your house. He needs to go to his room so he can rest. Please, move aside, sir."

"I will not be bossed around in my own house! I built this place from —"

"With all due respect, sir, I've personally met the contracting firm you hired. You *paid* for this house to be built from the ground up with the money your father gave you, which was likely born from money his father gave him. Now, if you'll excuse me, I really do need to get Simon to his room."

Simon opened his mouth to chime in, but he lost his train of thought. He *hated* how his dad talked to Leilani. It made his blood boil. And he couldn't tell if it was because of his dad's own anger, his racism, or his rage at Leilani telling him off that fueled it. Maybe it was a mixture of all three. That was a thought for sober Simon to figure out.

"You think you can wheedle in here? How do we even know those three weren't friends of yours and this is some sort of con? I've seen how y'all plan and—"

"What do you mean by 'y'all?'"

"What?"

Leilani's tone was pure ice. "I said, what do you mean by y'all?"

"You know what it means."

"Oh, I know it means 'you all.' And I want to know *who* you mean by that. Tell me. In exact words, who is 'you all' supposed to mean?"

"Now don't you try to twist my words—"

"I'm not twisting anything. I'm asking for clarification. Who. Is. Y'all?"

Dad drew in another deep breath, and Simon was busy

putting words together to tell him off when there was the sound of something metallic banging against the banister.

"What in high heaven is going on here? I sent my injured son to bed, so why is he not tucked in already?"

Ooooh, that was Mom and she sounded *angry. Very angry.*

"You have to stop—" Dad started, but it was very clear that Mrs. Miller was having none of it.

"You listen here, because I am only saying this once. You leave Leilani and the rest of the girls alone. You leave Simon alone. It's clear that you and I need to have a *very* serious discussion about many things, but right now I am tending to *our* son, who has been *stabbed*, so you will go to our space and ponder all the thoughts in your heart that make you feel like you need to act this way, do you understand? Because this is *not* the man I married, and I don't even feel like I know you anymore. Nor am I sure I want to."

There was silence for a moment, Mr. Miller looking like he wanted to say a whole lot but also completely horrified. Simon tried to twist his neck so he could see his mom, but she was too far down the stairs behind him and he couldn't quite figure out the mechanics of it.

And then, just like that, Dad walked away, leaving Leilani to continue guiding Simon to his food.

He was embarrassed, he realized faintly. Both at that she had to help him walk around his own house, but also because his dad had made a complete buffoon of himself. Simon hoped she didn't think *he* was like that, or that he held those beliefs in the back of his mind. Because he didn't.

Sure, Simon had a lot to learn about his own biases and felt like he was discovering new privileges he had every day, but he wanted to be good and loving and to shine as a beacon of equality for all. He didn't want to be like his dad or other small-minded people he'd met. He wanted to be *better.*

"Your mother is an incredible woman," Leilani murmured finally.

And Simon agreed fully with that. Sure, he and his brothers had their issues, but they probably would have been a lot worse without their mom. Their beautiful, smart, and kind of lonely mom.

Where was Auntie Kini? He was sure Mom could use some time venting to her closest friend. Maybe even put her feet up and have some tea. He went to ask Leilani if she knew where her Auntie was, only for an entirely different question to come out.

"Will you be my plus-one for Solomon's wedding coming up?"

They had stopped. Oh goodness, why had they stopped? Did she hate him? Had he offended her? Was she horrified?

She cleared her throat and he realized that they were at his door. Oh.

"Of course. It's the least I can do for the man who saved me."

"I didn't save you," he said, much less smoothly than he had with his brother. "Um, I gave you... just tools. Lotta tools."

"Simon, I realize you're coming off an adrenaline rush and drugged up to the gills from the medicine the ER gave you, but I hope you can remember how incredibly grateful I am for everything you've done." Like a dream, Leilani stood on tiptoes and pressed a whisper of a kiss against his cheek. "I trust that you can make it to your bed on your own?"

"Huh? Oh. Yeah, I can do that."

"Good. Thank you, Simon. I'll see you in the morning. I'm

sure your mom is going to want to spend the rest of the evening with you. She was worried about you, you know."

Simon nodded, and Leilani turned to head toward her own room in another hall. He watched her go, feeling warm and happy and like he'd slipped right out of reality into somewhere wonderful.

She was going to be his date *and* she'd kissed his cheek. It was more than he'd dared to hope for.

Chuckling at himself, Simon practically floated into his room. Things were changing. He could feel it.

15

———

Leilani

*L*eilani's opinions on law enforcement didn't improve all that much in the days following the setup. She was lucky that the two officers leading her case actually cared, and they were attentive to detail, meticulous in their paperwork, and in good communication with her and the Millers. The others, however... well, they left something to be desired. Like the cop at the precinct who had guided her to the interview room before making a comment about wasting police time that he either thought she couldn't hear or didn't care that she could. There was also the officer who had accompanied her to the lineup who made a comment about her "ex-boyfriend." Then there were the comments that were written in her files that the officers had to go over to make sure they weren't true. It was insulting what had been written about her back when she was a teenager, alone and scared.

But still, at least the three were arrested, Kai firmly in custody, and she had a taste of peace.

Her mother was elated, naturally, and started talking about Leilani coming home. But since the incident had happened in Texas, Kai was probably going to face justice in Texas, and she wanted to stick around to go to the trial if they needed her testimony. Besides, she was making a good amount of money, so it made sense to try to build up a lovely nest egg before going back home where jobs were less available and didn't pay as much while the cost of living was that much higher.

...and maybe she also didn't want to leave a certain cowboy.

It was strange, the transition her mind went through. Simon had always been on her radar, but he went from the mysterious man who she couldn't quite figure out and who avoided her like the plague, to literally the man who had turned her entire life around. Because of him, she could sleep at night. She didn't have to look over her shoulder, wondering if Kai was there. And for the first time since she was eighteen, she took a selfie outside then posted it to her social media.

It was like breathing for the first time after years of being underwater. Drinking after years of thirst. And she owed it all to Simon. A man who believed her and decided he wanted to do something about it.

After all that, she couldn't help but notice him more.

Because, as it turned out, he was all around, and she'd just never realized.

He was the one who turned on the coffee machine for Auntie Kini and his mom every morning, something she found out when she woke up early to surprise them by doing just that.

He was the one who refilled the fruit bowl if it got too low.

He brought out drinks to his brothers. He walked with his

mother in the garden. He read quietly outside or did things on his computer while Frenchie sketched him. He helped his brothers whenever they asked him, and he rode around on several different horses a couple of times a week.

So Leilani began to talk to him.

It was little things at first, asking how his wound was. If he rested well. What his horses' names were. And whenever they did talk, his eyes would crinkle in the corners and he would look at her in a way that she didn't entirely understand. A way that made her nervous and excited and hopeful all at once.

She was being silly.

Simon was handsome, rich, and strong. He could have his choice of any woman he wanted to. There was no way he could ever *really* be interested in her. Sure, he'd asked her out, but that had been before he'd seen her throw a punch, get fired, and found out about all the massive baggage she carried around. She was damaged goods, plain and simple.

But despite all that, after a week or so of talking, that turned into eating a couple of meals together a week. Whether it was lunch or snacks, or a dinner cooked by Mrs. Miller or spam musubi, they sat and talked with each other and whoever else was there.

It was nice.

And then that niceness became a routine.

So naturally, three weeks post-Kai, she walked into the kitchen at lunch expecting Simon there, only to find the young women of the Miller ranch there instead, papers and magazines spread out between them.

"Oh! Leilani!" Frenchie cried, nearly vaulting herself off of the stool she'd been perched on. Out of everyone on the ranch, she was the shortest, so it was always amusing to watch her scramble on furniture meant for people with a solid foot or two on her. "You're just the person I wanted to see!"

"I am?"

She nodded, already throwing her arms around her. "Yes! I heard that you're going to be a plus-one at my wedding! Is that true?"

"Uh, yeah, I think so."

"You think so?"

"Well, Simon was pretty out of it when he asked me."

"Not *that* out of it. He told Solomon a couple of days ago that you were going with him. Do you have anything to wear? At first, I really didn't care, but Solomon said he'd like it if the people who attended all wore warm, springy colors since our wedding palette is blue, black, and purple. Oh yeah, and white, of course."

"I, uh, I hadn't thought about it." While she had thought about Simon asking her to be his plus-one plenty, and how nervous he'd looked when he asked, she hadn't put much thought into the logistics of it. "I think I might have something. But if I don't, I can always go buy something."

"Wait, do you wanna go shopping for it? I can take you!" Frenchie's voice kicked up an octave. "Oh, please, if you don't mind. It would be so fun! We haven't gone shopping together for anything yet."

Elizabeth chuckled. "After years of never being able to, Frenchie is making up for lost time."

"Hey, there's a reason it's called retail *therapy*, and you weren't complaining when I went shopping for all those toys to donate to your animal fundraiser." Frenchie narrowed her eyes at Teddy next. "And you didn't complain when I went shopping for all of those rare plant starters at the jamboree-fest or the shindig."

"Hey," Teddy said, hands up. "I didn't say anything. I, for one, love when you spoil me."

"Yeah, that's right."

"I personally love it when you treat me to our fish fry dates every other Friday," Nova chipped in, her chin in her hand as she watched the whole conversation with a bemused expression. "Feel free to add any more meals onto that."

"You always think with your stomach," Frenchie teased. "It's why we get along." She looked to Leilani, her eyes full of excitement. "I'm trying to gain another dress size before my wedding, so if we go shopping, that means we can also get unhealthy food while we're at it."

"You want to gain weight?" Leilani asked quizzically. She was so used to people hating anything to do with fat that the idea surprised her.

But Frenchie just made a *tsk* sound. "Not everyone can be blessed with all that you've got going on, but I used to be a bit softer. Last year I finally got back to a size two, but I think around a four is where I'll feel healthiest, you know? And I want to be at my healthiest for my wedding."

"...and anything that comes right after the wedding," Nova said with a mischievous smile, resulting in Teddy elbowing her.

"Just be careful," Elizabeth said with a wan grin. "If you're a good guest, you're going to be invited to all of our weddings and Frenchie will drag you shopping each and every time."

"Wait, you're getting married too?" While Leilani knew that Teddy was engaged to Silas, she'd never heard Sterling or Elizabeth say anything about it.

"Yes. We've just been waiting for Solomon and Silas to pick dates so there's no stepping on anyone's toes."

"You mean like when Solomon proposed to Frenchie on Nova and Sal's one-year anniversary without even realizing it?"

"Yup."

They all shared a laugh together, and Leilani realized that she had a chance to integrate into a friend group without possibly endangering any of them.

"Okay," she said suddenly, startling them out of their mirth.

"Okay what?"

"Let's go shopping," Leilani said. "I'll clock out early and use some of my PTO. I assume that my bosses won't mind the excursion."

"Aw *yeah!*" Frenchie clapped her hands. "I'll go call Tawny and some others, see if they wanna come too. Gimme like... thirty minutes. If anyone else wants to come, now's the time to get ready!"

And that was how Leilani found herself heading to her first girls' day out since she was seventeen years old.

It was exhausting. It was wonderful. Her feet ached, her back hurt, and her nerves were frayed, but she loved every moment of it.

To her surprise, they didn't just go straight to some dress boutiques. They went shoe shopping first, and Leilani had *tried* to buy herself a pair, but before she knew it, Frenchie grabbed them out of her hands and paid for them while giving her a sly smile.

Next was some accessories. Leilani wasn't huge into jewelry because if it fell off, it would just get lost in the sand, but Frenchie picked out a bracelet and silver circlet with a peachy gem inside that was so delicate Leilani was almost afraid she'd break it.

"You don't think that this is too attention-grabbing?" Leilani asked, looking at herself in the small, round mirror. She looked like a magical enchantress or some sort of fantasy princess.

"Are you kidding me? With your hair down, this is going to

look *amaaay-zing.*" The tinier woman hummed, her hand cupping Leilani's cheek. She was surprisingly tactile, this Frenchie, and it reminded Leilani of her friends back home. A lot of the people on the mainland were very closed off physically, and platonic affection was almost nonexistent. It was nice to have a chance at that again.

Frenchie's voice softened, bringing Leilani back to the moment. "You know, I used to dream of being able to treat my friends like this. To buy them nice things just because I wanted to see them smile. It's been over three years, and it hasn't gotten any less brilliant."

Leilani thought of all the nice things that she had been able to buy Auntie Kini since her paycheck and hours had both increased. She thought of being able to send her family way more money back home. And yeah, she knew exactly how good that feeling was.

"Thank you, Frenchie," she said, and then the trinkets were hers.

They saved the dress for last, and Leilani dreaded it. Unlike shoes or jewelry, it was much harder to find something in her size. But then Teddy was taking over, and they walked to a tucked-away boutique off the main drag of expensive shops. She and a girl named Tawny were linked arm and arm, singing some sort of hip-hop song that Leilani wasn't familiar with. She didn't listen to the radio all that much now that her hour and fifteen-minute commute had transitioned into a five-minute walk from the Miller's mansion to their fields.

But to her great surprise, there were plenty of plus-size options in the store. In fact, it seemed to be mostly plus-size options and all high quality. Nothing frumpy or grandma-ish. Leilani had no idea how a shop like that existed, but she happily went about trying on different dresses until she found something that made Frenchie clap and Teddy give a low whistle.

"You know, I'm not used to having competition for someone else with my figure," she remarked with a grin. "But *wow*, you look good."

"You don't think it's too much?" Leilani asked. While she loved her body most of the time, she was aware that certain cuts looked more... salacious on her than it would on someone with a more svelte figure.

"No, not at all," Frenchie said, eyeing her with only a hint of jealousy in her eyes. "If anything, this motivates me to make sure I keep eating and working out. Gosh, you're so pretty." The last part was said almost wistfully, and Leilani knew that tone anywhere.

"I know literally thousands of people who would kill for a body like yours," Leilani said. And she meant it. She'd seen Frenchie in a bathing suit, the girl was all muscle and sinew, with abs and hardly an ounce of fat on her. She wasn't skeletal, or even unhealthy looking, just thin.

"I don't care about what other people want. I want what *I* want, which is to look like I used to before... well, you know, life happened."

Leilani nodded. "I understand. I think you're beautiful, but I want you to be happy with your body too."

"Girl, same. I'll fill out my wedding dress like a champ, you just watch. Now, who wants to go load up on carbs and protein?"

There was a sound of agreement all around and Leilani wondered if she would ever stop smiling.

~

WHEN LEILANI MADE it back home—since when was she thinking of it as *home*?—she was thoroughly tired but more excited than ever about the wedding. She'd had no idea it was in just five weeks. The whole house seemed awfully calm about it, but apparently that was because Solomon had been tucking away details, planning and sending queries to different businesses that they would need ever since he'd given Frenchie a promise ring.

The whole gaggle of them entered the main house, laughing and talking, their cheeks red and their feet barking, but all of that came to a halt when Mrs. Miller appeared from the main sitting area with a serious look on her face.

"Leilani, may I talk to you?"

Everyone knew that tone couldn't possibly be a good one, and Leilani swallowed hard. "Yes, of course."

"I'll put your bags up in your room," Frenchie offered quietly. "We'll be around for a while if you want to talk later."

"Yeah. Okay."

Leilani felt apprehension roll up her spine, and that feeling only increased tenfold as Mrs. Miller led her to what looked like a study, where the private investigator and Simon were already sitting.

"What happened?" she said, freezing stock-still in the doorway. She couldn't enter the room, she couldn't. It already felt like she could hardly breathe. That warm, happy feeling was gone, replaced with a cold, bitter sort of scorn for her daring to believe that things could go good for once.

"Apologies, Miss Cunningham," the man said, standing and offering her his hand. She just stared at it, knowing she was being rude, but she couldn't help it.

"What *happened*?"

"Right. Well, as you know, all three of your assailants were arrested and in jail. Unfortunately, while two of them are still here, Kai himself made his bail as of three days ago. He was behaving himself, responding to his parole officer, and he had an ankle monitor. However... as of this afternoon, his ankle monitor's tamper alarm went off. By the time officers got to his location, he was gone. They tried to find him, but—and I truly am sorry about this—but he's in the wind. I will continue trying to find him, but as of right now, he's completely ghosted us."

With every word out of his mouth, the roaring in Leilani's ears increased until she could barely hear him. Kai was free. Kai was out and Kai was free, and they had no idea where Kai was. Her ever-present shadow was loose, the monster under her bed ready to snatch her up again.

...when was it ever going to end?

16

―――――

Simon

Three weeks passed and Simon's wound was almost gone, the stitches taken out after the tenth day when the itching was the worst. He still felt it catch a little if he turned the wrong way, but all in all, he was good as new.

Maybe even better because his relationship with Leilani had completely changed. At first, they talked every day, and those conversations were bright points that he latched onto and looked forward to. Then it turned into meals together or with family, talking and laughing and enjoying each other's company.

She didn't shy away from him; she actively seemed to seek him out. And although they never talked about Kai, it was clear that she felt safer when Simon was around.

And he could live with that.

But the closer she became to him, the more they talked, the

more Simon wanted. Parting from her was like ripping a bandage off, except there was no relief until he was back in her presence again, listening to her laugh or joke.

He didn't know when he had gotten it so bad, but it was clear to him that his attachment went beyond attraction. He had the deepest, most virulent crush that he'd ever had, and he didn't want to ever climb out of it.

It burned hotter whenever she was being hyper-cautious or scared, flooding him with the desire to protect her. It bubbled whenever she told him a story about her past, happy that he was learning more about her. It fizzled and popped whenever she told a funny joke and *man*, did he *laugh*.

It was just so *good*. It figured. He'd wandered around the entire world trying to find himself, and yet he'd never felt more grounded than in her presence back home on the ranch.

"You've got that dopey look on your face again," Sal said, chuckling.

"Do I?" Simon drawled, not caring in the least. There was a time, not too long ago, where he would have denied it, but what was the point? He had it bad for Leilani, even if she didn't seem to see him as a romantic figure at all.

But that was okay. He was happy being her friend. It wasn't like that was a consolation prize. He was happy that he ever got to talk with her, make her laugh.

Still... he wouldn't mind... *more*.

"Yeah, you definitely do. You going steady with Leilani yet?"

"No. We haven't even gone on a single date." He urged his horse ahead, not realizing that he had fallen behind from his brothers. They'd all decided to go on a horse ride together, going around the outside of their property at a slow pace.

None of them said it, but Simon knew what they were thinking. They all wanted to run a perimeter, make sure their loved ones were safe. No one knew where Kai was, and his presence lingered in the air like a rotten stench. Simon appreciated that all of his brothers were so willing to help and didn't seem to blame Leilani at all. Not like their dad.

Thinking of his dad just made Simon grip his reins harder. He hadn't seen the man since he'd come home all stitched and drugged up, but just remembering it made his blood boil. He hoped that he had been so inebriated that he'd imagined some of the awful things his dad had said, but when he brought it up with either Leilani or his mom, they'd usually change the subject.

"Why not? You've clearly got it bad for her."

"Never would have thought I'd see independent Simon tethered to the ground by one woman," Solomon remarked ruefully. "It's something to see."

"You lot are *so* hilarious. As if you weren't all sworn single and anti-relationship before running into your ladies."

"Never said I wasn't," Solomon shot back. "But you're the one doing it last, so now we all get to make fun of you."

"Great. Hilarious."

"But on a serious note," Silas said, dropping back carefully on Amaranth. The older twin's horse had been healed for a while, but he still rode so cautiously atop her. "Why haven't you asked her out? It's okay if you're not ready, but *is* there a reason?"

"Well, I figured I'd wait for the wedding, ya know? Figured I don't really have another option for a plus-one if I tick her off, so why risk it?"

"Have you seen the way Leilani looks at you? That's not exactly what I would call a risk."

Simon looked sharply to Sterling. "What? She looks at me?"

Both of the twins let out a derisive snort. "Is the sky blue?"

Sterling answered. "Yeah, she looks at you. All the time. With those big gray eyes of hers, and sometimes I can't tell if she wants to kiss you or dissect you."

Wait, what? Was that even a good thing? "Uh... thanks? I guess?"

"Don't worry about it," Sterling said more comfortingly. "From what I've heard about things, Leilani's missed out on a lot of things that would be normal for a young lady to experience. She's probably just figuring things out as much as you are."

Simon had to concentrate on his mind not chasing down that rabbit hole, because it would. Ever since the day where he'd found out about Kai, he'd never read a single additional word from the files. He figured that was Leilani's personal information and that she would tell him when she was ready. Which clearly, she wasn't.

But it was all too easy for him to imagine the awful things that could have happened. And if he did start doing that, he would get angry all over again, thinking about worse and worse things until he was sick from it.

"Yeah. Probably."

"Hey, it's getting later and Mom's in the city for a charity function. What if we had a bonfire?" Sal said, rubbing his chin. "We could invite everyone, so that would give you a chance to hang out with Leilani without any pressure. It wouldn't be a date, it'd just be a group hang out."

Simon beamed at his brother. "And they say you're all brawn and no brains."

"What, who says that?"

But Simon's mind was already racing off. "Alright, you all text your ladies and then I'm certain Nova will text Leilani.

Does anyone know if we have s'mores ingredients in the pantry?"

"We *always* have stuff for s'mores in the pantry," Silas said.

Simon found himself grinning so widely his cheeks hurt. "A bonfire it is, then."

THE IDEA of the bonfire had sounded so nice, but once it happened and they were all gathered, Simon realized that he and Leilani were the only single ones there. And while that normally wouldn't be too big of an issue, it was painfully obvious once everyone started to couple off and roast marshmallows together.

No one was making out, of course, but they had their arms around each other, kisses were pressed to cheeks and heads were leaned against shoulders. It was all very cozy and romantic, which made Simon wonder why he ever agreed—even encouraged—the outing.

But a gentle hand on his arm from Leilani had him singing a different tune.

"This is nice," she said with a soft smile, gray eyes on him. "I haven't had a bonfire since Hawaii."

"Really?" he asked, surprised. Bonfires were practically a rite of passage.

She nodded. "We used to have them on the beach, me and my friends, or me and my coworkers. Sometimes it was me and my family. We loved to look up at the stars. I was pretty good at cooking things on them, although usually we just brought snacks and had fun. I missed it."

"I'm glad we can do this for you, then."

She affixed him with a mischievous sort of smile that sent his blood rushing. "Oh, so this is all for me?"

"I can neither confirm nor deny that."

"Uh-huh, that says more than you know."

"Does it now?"

She was regarding him with that *look* again. The one that made him want to show off but also stand perfectly still so he couldn't somehow mess it up.

"Oh yeah, it does."

"Glad I'm so easy to read."

"In some ways," she said, her grin growing. "In other ways, not so much. Pass the marshmallows, please."

His hands automatically did what she asked, but his eyes never left her face. Goodness, he could stare at that face forever. The roundness of her apple cheeks, the almond shape of her eyes. The way her broad nose led to those plump lips colored somewhere between terracotta and deep umber. He wanted to press his thumb against them, trace their lines until he had them memorized. Maybe press his lips against them too...

"Chocolate."

"Pardon?"

"Could you pass me the chocolate?"

He did so, swallowing hard. He needed to concentrate and get his mind in order. The last thing he wanted to do was make Leilani uncomfortable when she'd already been through so much.

"You ever had a s'more with peanut butter cups?"

"No, I haven't. Have you?"

"Oh yeah, I've tried *lots* of different sweets with smores. Kit Kats, toffee, cookies n' cream. They all have pros and cons. Well, cookies n' cream is mostly cons. You know it's not actually chocolate? It's just cream, butter, and sugar, but they started calling it white chocolate to boost its sales way back when and, wouldn't you know, it worked."

Simon had never been more interested in chocolate in his whole life. "Huh, just needed some rebranding then, I guess."

"Yeah, sometimes folks just need to see things in a different light."

There was something in her tone that made that sentence have weight. Simon couldn't put his finger on it, but those words sank right down into his heart and stayed there for him to think about later.

"Ah! No! I burned half of mine. You distracted me."

"Did I?" Simon said, trying to sound charming, but he had a feeling that he wasn't quite there.

"Yeah! Now it's all burnt. See?"

She held out her marshmallow to him. It was a dark brown, golden toward the top.

"What are you talking about? That's practically perfect," he said.

"Ew, no. I like it golden all around and gooey-melty. Not hard on the outside or that hot."

"Fine, then I'll eat it."

"Will you?"

"Yeah, never want to let food go to waste, after all."

He couldn't interpret the look she gave him as she took the chocolate and graham cracker from her lap and carefully pieced together the campfire confection. He expected her to hand it to him, maybe make a quip or two, but instead she held the morsel out to him, the tips of her fingers gingerly compressing the middle.

"Go on," she said, sounding a bit breathless. "Take a bite."

He looked from her, to the treat she was offering, and back. In reality, he knew it could probably be a fairly innocuous gesture, but to him it seemed like so much more. Like it had weight. Like once he reached out for that treat, they would be crossing a line that couldn't be uncrossed.

But Leilani held it steadily, looking at him with half-lidded eyes. After another full beat, he slowly leaned forward and let his mouth close around half of the treat.

He hadn't meant to, but his lips brushed against her fingers as he did so, ever so slightly. They were cool to the touch and set the skin of his face alight like she'd shocked him. She hadn't, of course, but suddenly everything was amplified, from the crunch of his teeth through the graham cracker to how the marshmallow coated his tongue in warm sugar.

Their eyes remained locked the entire time, even when he pulled back to chew. He hardly paid attention to what his mouth did, his whole mind locked on Leilani and only Leilani.

And she seemed just as caught up in him. Her eyes roamed his face, settling on his mouth as he chewed. Eventually, when he managed to swallow it down, her gaze traced the path of his tongue as he licked his lips.

They were leaning toward each other, both of them hardly breathing, entirely caught up in what was happening.

Until a giant grasshopper landed on what remained of the sugary treat in Leilani's hand.

"Ah! Get it off!"

Before Simon could do anything of the sort, Leilani threw the s'more wildly, only for it to smack into Sal's shoulder.

"Um, did I do something wrong?"

"Sorry!" Leilani said in a panic. "There was a massive bug."

Simon couldn't hold it in anymore, they'd gone from a serious, intense moment to slapstick comedy and the transition was too much for him. He pressed his hand to his mouth, trying to hold his chuckling in, but then Leilani made eye contact and they were both laughing.

"Did... did I miss something?" Nova asked from Sal's lap. "There was a bug and now you two are howling."

Simon just shook his head, waving away the question as the warm fire soaked through him. He felt content in a way he hadn't in ages, the ghost of Kai forgotten for just a few moments.

He should have known the moment couldn't last.

"So, since we're all here," Solomon started, low voice pulling the attention of their group to him. "I didn't want to say anything before, just in case, but I can safely say that I've been in contact with a majority of the board members one on one and they're in agreement that it's time to make a change in our mission statement and are prepared to 'encourage' Dad to retire. It will give him a chance to destress with Mom and finally allow us to make some of the bigger changes that we've been wanting."

...what?

"Are you serious?" Sterling asked, surprise lacing his tone. "You really got those crusty old men to agree?"

"I don't think it would have happened if Dillinger hadn't retired last year and his son was put in his place, or if Mather's hadn't had a stroke, but you'd be surprised that a couple of them are far more progressive than we'd thought. Besides, I knew how to pare things down to money to make them seem more advantageous."

Silas let out a whistle. "Are you sure about this? Because this is going to draw a line in the sand even more than ever."

"How can I not be? Dad's resisting us at every turn. He still won't budge on those contracts supplying parts from oversees when we've presented him proof of child labor. He's still fighting us on getting our workers all the benefits they need. He's still using profits from the company for all of his political machinations. And if anything, his behavior is escalating in a way to try to counteract us. Did you know he'd reached out to the Barringtons about starting another warehouse not far from Teddy's neighborhood? Put in speculations for entire blocks all around the area."

"He what?" Teddy asked sharply, sitting up from where she'd been curled in Silas's lap. "If that man thinks he can touch our neighborhoods with his—"

"That sounds like a coup," Simon cut in, and suddenly all eyes were on him.

"Pardon?" Solomon said.

"I said, what you're talking about basically sounds like a coup."

They were quiet for a moment, before Solomon answered, his words careful. "Well, I guess it is." His gaze then moved to the rest of them. "Look, I realize we owe our dad everything. If we didn't win the lotto of being born to him, we wouldn't have met who we've met, or done the things we've managed to do. We live comfortable, incredible lives because of him.

"But for the past fifteen years, we've all been complacent, content, and let money be our god. We can't live like that anymore. And since Dad refuses to listen and has only grown more and more angry, we're left with no choice."

There was a chorus of agreements all around, with everyone promising their hand to help, but Simon stayed quiet. His brother was right. In fact, he agreed with him on almost everything he said. But ousting their dad from the empire that he created... well... it just seemed far too political for him. So instead he made another s'more and hoped no one asked him anything.

He wasn't sure if it was a good or a bad thing when another hour passed, and no one did.

17

———————

Leilani

*I*t was the day of the wedding!

It wasn't even her wedding and yet she was awash with nerves, checking herself over and over again in the video feed on her phone while she talked to her family. Without them and Auntie Kini with her, she was sure that she would have spent the entire morning in a tizzy.

"So, when is *your* wedding, Leilani? You come back home for that, right, when you are all rich and famous?"

"*Mom.* I'm just his plus-one. It's not even a date."

"A mother knows these things," her mom said. "I can smell it in the air. My baby is too beautiful for these cowboys to resist."

"*Mom.*" Leilani rolled her eyes. Her mother was eccentric and loved to tease, but Leilani didn't know what she'd do without her. "Let's not get ahead of ourselves, alright. And let's definitely not talk about money. It's bad enough his father only thinks I'm around to try to dig at his family's money."

"That man. His wife must be a miracle worker to make sons who are decent people."

Leilani nodded, distracted as she put lipstick on in the mirror. She didn't own a ton of makeup since she came to the mainland, too bulky to bring with and too expensive to buy, but Frenchie had apparently amassed quite the supply and had given Leilani some of her duplicates or things she didn't want anymore. Although, Leilani got the feeling that Frenchie actually had a stockpile of makeup specifically to give away to people but didn't want to admit it.

"When are *you* going to get a boyfriend?" Auntie Kini cut in, leaning into the phone camera. Malia and Leilani's youngest brother laughed, looking to their mom expectantly. "You haven't dated either this whole time, right? Pot calling kettle black?"

Mom huffed. "No one asked you, Auntie Kini. Just let me bother my daughter in peace."

"Ah-ah, turnabout is fair play."

It was all said with smiles and laughter, their family banter like a warm, familiar blanket in the background of Leilani's anxiety.

She just wanted to look nice for Simon. She hadn't been able to get that moment at the bonfire out of her head ever since it happened. She didn't know what had come over her, but one moment she was making a s'more, the next she was feeding Simon out of her hand, his lips brushing the very tips of her fingers like a kiss while he stared into her eyes.

Wow.

It had been a moment alright.

And she had no idea what to do with it.

Ever since Kai, she hadn't felt anything romantic, not even so much as a speck of a crush. She spent all of her time blocking out everything that had happened or being terrified of being caught, so anything remotely like dating or a relationship always made her blood run cold. But she found herself... wanting. Or at least beginning to want, in a way she hadn't thought possible.

Like what would it feel like if Simon had kissed her? She knew it wouldn't be anything like Kai, who had been forceful, boxing her in, all teeth and mean words. She remembered how he used to bite her lip, hard, when she tried to end things before he was ready. Everything had always been about *him*.

But Simon wouldn't be anything like that. She knew that down into her soul. And so her soul wondered what it might be like to be with someone who didn't want to hurt her, own her, claim her.

"Are you alright, baby? You've gone pale."

"I'm fine," Leilani said quickly, her face heating up, returning to the real world. "Just thinking."

"What you thinkin' 'bout to make those cheeks so red, huh?"

"Oy, rest it. Let's get your shoes on and your circlet over your hair, shall we Leilani?"

Leilani nodded, letting her Auntie Kini put on the final touches. Once that was all done, the older woman stood back and let out a happy sigh.

"You look beautiful. Here, let me take a picture."

The woman pulled out one of those older digital cameras from who knew where and snapped a couple of shots of Leilani sitting there on the edge of the bed. Leilani certainly *did* think she looked nice, and she stood to go look in the full-length bathroom mirror to be sure.

Oh yeah, she looked *nice*.

She was wearing a knee-length, coral dress that went just an inch below her knees, Cuban stockings and bright, matching wedges that wouldn't do her wrong on the dance floor. Her hair was loose for once, tumbling down her shoulders and back in great big waves that mimicked the waters she hailed from. Her décolletage was bare save for the highlight that she'd used, but the bangle at her wrist reflected light everywhere while the circlet twinkled demurely in her dark, dark tresses.

Her makeup was subtle, as she only knew a few basic techniques, but it had her gray eyes popping and her full lips accentuated, her high cheekbones emphasized for a little extra boost. She looked like a princess, for the lack of a better word. Or at least the type of princess she'd always imagined being as a child.

...would Simon like it?

Normally she couldn't give two potatoes about what someone thought of her clothes or her figure or her look, but she found a small voice inside of her that very much wanted him to like her ensemble. That wanted him to tell her she was beautiful and lovely and good. To look at her how he'd looked at her during the bonfire, all open desire and appreciation.

Geez... somehow, in just a few short weeks, she'd gotten it bad, hadn't she.

Maybe that wouldn't have happened if it had just been the bonfire, but they'd continued to interact since. Continued to eat meals together. Continued to exist and talk together until she knew more about him than she ever did before. And with every story he told her, she felt more open to the idea that she could maybe.

Possibly.

Potentially.

Be in love.

...but what if she was *wrong*?

There was the thought that always ended up hitting her like a deluge of cold water and those warm, fuzzy thoughts spiraled away, drowned out by all the misery and fear that Kai had managed to plant and grow in her. Even when he was gone, he still did so much to rule her life. She hated it.

"Come on, dear. It's time to get you downstairs. I'm sure your lovely date is waiting for you."

"It's not a date," Leilani countered her auntie with absolutely no conviction.

Arm in arm, the two walked downstairs together, bidding goodbye to Leilani's family and ending the video call. It was impossible not to feel like some refined debutant as they walked down the stairs together, headed for the foyer.

Where of course Simon was standing by the door, texting with his head down. Even though she couldn't see his face, she could see how handsome he looked in his tan suit and mint tie. It wasn't a combination she was used to seeing on any of the Miller boys, but it certainly matched the warm color pallet that Frenchie had asked their attendees to wear.

He must have heard her as they approached the last few steps because his head tilted up to her, a smile on his face. And it was what happened right after that that let her know he *definitely* liked her get up.

First off, his rapidly moving thumbs froze and his phone slipped from his grasp, the man jerking to action and catching it before it hit the floor. When he straightened, she watched his Adam's apple bob as he swallowed, and his eyes roved all over her figure, never staying in one place for too long. Even his cheeks were coloring, making his bone structure look that much more blessed.

"You look... beautiful," he breathed, that grin back again but looking that much more sheepish. "I feel underdressed."

"A man should always feel underdressed in the company of a beautiful lady," Auntie Kini said teasingly, handing Leilani off so smoothly that the young woman didn't even quite realize what was happening until Simon's arm was entwined with hers.

"Now, not that I'm not grateful, but why is it you're not in the wedding party again? Leilani never really explained it."

Trust her auntie to find a time to get more info in that she absolutely didn't need to know. But Simon didn't seem to mind, smiling as he answered. "Solomon's always been more of a low-key kind of man and really only wanted a best man, and that's it. Frenchie's friends are most of the wedding party.

"Some people might be miffed at it, but I've got four other brothers. The way we figured, there will be plenty of chances to be in each other's wedding parties."

"Aw, well isn't that nice. All of you so considerate of each other." She patted Simon's cheek familiarly. "Now, off with you. I believe Nova will be here to pick me up any moment and I'm supposed to be the last one out of the house."

"Hah, alright. Be safe, Auntie."

They headed out of the door arm in arm, and Leilani got that magical, floaty feeling again. She tried not to blush but had a feeling she failed when Simon let her go only to open the door of his truck for her then offered a hand to help her up.

"Well, you ready to see Frenchie officially become your sister-in-law?" she asked once he was in and starting the car up.

"I'm ready to see my brother marry the love of his life."

Oh.

As if that wasn't an answer and a half.

THE WEDDING WAS BEAUTIFUL, what else could be expected from Frenchie? It was being held in one of the state parks that was known for holding weddings, a semi indoor / outdoor event with plenty of shade from a pavilion and trees, with the wedding party on some sort of a raised dais. There were blue, black, purple, and white flowers all over, some in beautiful vases, some bound together in garlands, and even some wound into a beautiful canopy that shaded the officiant and the bride and groom.

It was so *lovely*.

Leilani recognized about half of the faces in the small attendants. Considering the Millers were still a part of high society, she expected the guest list to be a real who's-who. But instead, a lot of it was workers or people who looked to be more around Leilani's class of folks. There was Tawny, of course, and a few people that were just familiar enough that Leilani was pretty sure she'd served them at her diner, but not enough for her to remember anything about them.

And, unsurprisingly, the warm color scheme looked brilliant compared to the cool colors of the wedding party, emphasizing them beautifully. The music was lovely, a combination of southern classics and romantic Latin songs gently drifting from the live band until the wedding march started.

Then, finally, Frenchie was coming out. She looked *beautiful*, dressed from head to toe in white lace, tailored to her body in a mermaid cut that flared around her feet in a glorious burst of fabric. Her hair had been done, dyed a pretty sort of auburn and styled in a beautiful updo that made her look a bit taller.

Leilani didn't know what the woman was worried about, she looked like a *dream*. Like a fairy queen elegantly floating down the purple carpet, beautiful and serene.

Then came their vows. And *wow*, if that wasn't something that made the corners of Leilani's eyes tear up.

"Francesca, when I first met you, it's safe to say you took my breath away. That might have been because I was chasing you halfway across the city and you had to vault a fence to get away from me."

There was a titter from the crowd. Leilani had never heard *that* particular story. She still had so much to learn about the Millers.

"Little did I know you were going to change my world forever. I didn't know it at the time, but I was trapped in the tiniest of boxes. Sure, that was living, but really, I was just going through the motions of life. You opened my eyes to so much more, and I can honestly say that I am a better man because of you.

"My heart has grown, my mind has grown, and when I look at you, I fall even more in love every day. I can't wait for a future with you, and everything we will learn together."

And then Frenchie spoke, her normally strong, charismatic voice trembling slightly.

"Solomon, when I first met you, I was scared. And angry. I was so used to fighting for every little scrap of anything I had that I didn't know what to do when you showed up and suddenly wanted to help me.

"But you showed me kindness like I'd never known before. You taught me that, while there is plenty of evil in the world, there is also good if you look for it. If you nurture it. It's because of you that my best friend in the world is alive. It's because of you that I've got an education that I thought I'd never have. It's because of you that I have hope for a better tomorrow, a better future, and the room to dream bigger than I ever thought possible.

"I can't wait for all we can do together; all we can change. I look forward to growing in love and maturity with you, every step of the way, growing stronger together."

Leilani sniffled, her heard aching in the best way possible. Looking at Solomon and Frenchie together, it was easy to see the love pouring out of them. She knew without a doubt that the man had never laid a hand on Frenchie, never tried to cut her down or force anything on her. She also knew that Frenchie had her own awful experience, had been hurt and mistreated.

If she could find love. If she could find a happily ever after, maybe Leilani could too.

Wouldn't that be something?

She heard other sniffs and murmurs around her, and it was comforting to know that she wasn't the only one affected. It was rare that a moment of pure *good* could be shared by so many folks, and Leilani reveled in it.

But what she wasn't expecting was for Simon's hand to slide into hers, his warm fingers sliding between her own. She looked to him, knowing there were still tears in her eyes, but he just smiled softly at her.

"Beautiful, right?"

She nodded, but with the way he was looking at her, her mind couldn't quite tell if he was talking about the vows, or *her*. And if that didn't just go straight to her heart.

The officiant had been talking, but Leilani only zoned in when it came to the part that everybody knew. It was a traditional phrase, and one Leilani wouldn't ever want in her wedding—if she ever was to be married, that was.

"If any of you has a reason why these two should not be married, speak now, or forever hold your peace."

Leilani loved drama, and she loved the trope in movies, but in real life, it just seemed needless and asking for trouble. At least nothing was—

"I have something to say!"

No.

No, no, no, no, no!

Leilani's whole body reacted, tensing so hard her back popped. Slowly, she turned around, to see Kai standing at the beginning of the purple rug.

He was dressed in a white tux, looking dapper and polished like a Prince Charming. He held a truly massive bouquet in his hand comprised of lilies and hibiscus, Leilani's favorite flowers.

"I'm sorry to interrupt your beautiful ceremony here, but I hope you understand I had to do this," he said, stepping forward as he projected his voice. "Because I'm just a man in love, and I can't risk losing the other half of my heart without trying."

Oh no. He wasn't... he wasn't...

"Leilani Cunningham, I am not a perfect man. I've done wrong, I've lost my temper and I was young and thick-headed when we first met. I understand now I squandered your affection and I don't deserve so much to have you look at me."

Squander? Who even said squander? Kai didn't talk like that. It was clear that he was putting on a show for the audience that didn't know them, and she was horrified that some of them bought into it.

"But I've changed. I learned, and I've even gotten my degree. I know you have no reason to trust me, but please, don't shut me out, Leilani. You're the perfect woman, and I love you with all of my heart. All I want is a chance to talk to you, to prove that I love you.

"I know you're with these people who don't think much of me or people who look like me, but don't let them change who you are, Leilani. You've always been this amazing, beautiful and fiery woman who was never afraid to speak up for yourself. Can you blame me for missing you?"

Lies. It was all lies. Part of Leilani wanted to hunker down into her seat, to just melt into the floor and pretend that she wasn't there at all. But so much of her was also churning with anger. How *dare* Kai try to make himself out to be a victim, ignored by a woman who ran off with people who discriminated against him. How dare he come and try to make Frenchie and Solomon's perfect day all about him. It was all so *awful.*

"I know they say it is better to have loved and lost than to not love at all, but please, Leilani, don't let me lose you. I can see a whole future together, but it's not the same without you in it."

That was the last straw. Leilani jumped up, unsure of what she would shout but knowing well enough that it was going to be *something* scathing, but Simon was already on his feet and slipping out of the line of seats.

"For all of you being charmed by this man and his story now," he said, voice calm, almost amiable. "Don't be. He's a lying snake, and he's trying to manipulate you to put pressure on Leilani to leave with him.

"But Leilani will not be leaving with him today. If any of you knew how much this woman has gone through to try to get away from his monster, all of you would be moving to kick him out right now."

Simon looked to Kai and the tension radiating off the both

of them was palpable. "You're not welcome here, Kai. You're not welcome in Leilani's life or even in Texas. Get out of here, because I'm sure the cops have already been called."

"I—"

"No!"

Leilani jolted when Frenchie's voice cut in, hot and sharp and powerful.

"Enough of this. This man *stabbed* my brother-in-law and has threatened my friend over and over again. And now he's escaped from police custody."

"Technically slashed," Simon murmured.

But Frenchie just went right on going, stomping down the dais with her finger pointed. "You are a coward, Kai, a miserable, lonely, ugly little monster of a man, and you are not welcome here! You're not going to ruin my wedding day and you're not getting Leilani, so get *out!*"

There was a murmur of shock through the crowd, people glancing uncertainly between all the parties involved. Leilani *hated* that all of this was about her and Kai's calculations were right, she did want to go with him just to avoid a scene. Because they were absolutely in a scene at the moment.

Movement from the wedding party drew Leilani's attention, and she saw Teddy was already on her phone, talking urgently to someone who Leilani presumed was the police. Sal and Sterling were also standing up and edging out of the row of seats they were in.

And that was when it hit Leilani, really hit Leilani.

She wasn't alone.

Sure, she'd always had her family. She'd always had her Auntie Kini. But now she had so much *more*. There was Nova, with her long legs and easy smile who loved sharing memes and taught Leilani almost everything she knew about her job.

There was Teddy who shared her tailor with Leilani, and they'd started shopping online together and sharing fashion inspo texts. There was Elizabeth, kind and gentle and reserved but always ready to answer any question. Silas. Sterling. Sal. Solomon. Mrs. Miller.

And of course, Simon.

They were all there, on her side, never blaming her for what had happened or what Kai had done to her. They backed her up. They *believed* her. They didn't think she was dumb or a vixen or asked for any of it. Didn't think she was dramatic.

She didn't have to be scared anymore.

That made courage bubble up in her, bright and full of hope. Before she knew it, words were pouring out of her mouth too.

"It's over. I have no feelings for you and I never will. You've hurt me, Kai. You've hurt me more than any person should be hurt, and if you don't leave me alone, you're going to end up in prison for your whole life. And I can't be worth that, Kai. No one can. Move on and live your life while you still can, because I'm putting my foot down."

She could see the fissures form in Kai's façade, splintering that perfect Prince Charming veneer. "Aw, come off it, LeiLei. You don't mean that. These *haoles* got you all confused and turned inside out."

"I've never been more clear in my entire life. Go, Kai. Right now."

"You know, you say this now. But I can go home, yeah?" His tone turned sickeningly sweet, the way it always did before he did something that made her feel awful. She remembered how she used to be so afraid of that tone and what he would do. Not anymore. She was so tired of being afraid. "Maybe I say hi to your family there, see how they're doing without you, huh?

Maybe *they'll* be nice to me. Malia is growing up to be prettier than you, I think. Not letting herself become some fat who—"

There was a blur of movement, and suddenly Simon had closed the distance between them, decking Kai right across the face.

Kai stumbled back, clearly not having expected the move, and Simon followed up with another hit that had him flat on his back, his eyes fluttered closed. Leilani had never seen Kai get bested in a fight, and she was pretty sure that if he hadn't been staring at her, then Simon wouldn't have been able to get the drop on him.

"Here," Leilani said, handing him the pretty pashmina that she had donned for the sunniest part of the ceremony.

Simon took it from her, hog-tying the man with it. Kai awoke somewhere in the middle of the process, yelling obscenities and threatening things, but he was well and truly bound.

By the time Simon finished, Sal was striding forward, and together the two of them hauled Kai out. And hopefully out of Leilani's life forever.

Once the brothers finished dragging him out of the ceremonial space and back toward the cars, Leilani realized that all eyes were on her. Her heart squeezed, guilt bubbling up like usual, but someone gently cleared their throat behind her.

Thankfully, attention went to the source of the sound: Frenchie.

"Well, that was a fun intermission, but if y'all don't mind, spotlight back on us. After all, Solomon has been awfully patient waiting for me to be ready for this day."

There was a small wave of uncertain laughter and things started to settle down. Frenchie took to the dais, gripping Solomon's outstretched hand. The man didn't look like he could be prouder, face practically glowing.

And just like that, the ceremony got started up again, and everything started to settle out. One thing was for certain, Frenchie and Solomon were going to have one heck of a wedding story to tell people.

It took a minute for the officiant to get his rhythm back, but when he did, it was like nothing had ever happened at all, and somehow, Simon made it back to his seat before the big kiss, his hand sliding into hers just as his brother began to say his "I dos."

Leilani was pretty sure that there wasn't a dry eye in the house after both parties exchanged rings and choked out loving promises to be each other's forever, and then the minister was saying those special words.

"You may kiss the bride."

The cheer that came up was incredible, like all the tension and drama from before was being transmuted into only positive, perfect happiness. And perhaps Leilani cheered the loudest, because as Solomon kissed Frenchie so tenderly, Leilani could see a brand-new chapter opening up in all of their lives.

18

Simon

Simon clapped hard as his brother kissed his new wife for the very first time in their marriage. It was so wholesome, so perfectly perfect that he couldn't help but be moved by it. He'd traveled around the world, thought he was so learned, so much *better* than his siblings with their small worlds and their hometown fiancées, but he had been wrong.

So very, very wrong.

All of their worlds had been small before, including his, because their worlds were always wrapped only around themselves and what they wanted. But Frenchie, Teddy, Elizabeth, Nova, and Leilani had opened their eyes, forced them to look at themselves and expand. And as Simon sat there, his leg pressed against Leilani's soft one, he couldn't help but be incredibly grateful to her. She didn't even know all that she had done for him. Not even a little.

Because for the past few weeks, he hadn't felt that aching void. Hadn't felt purposeless, useless, or adrift. He hadn't felt *empty*. No, he'd needed to protect her, to defend her, or even just listen to her. And that feeling had only grown and grown with each passing day.

He just hoped that, this time around, prison stuck. He'd called the PI almost as soon as they were far away from the ceremony, Kai still screaming threats, and the man had assured him that hopping bail pretty much put a nail in the guy's coffin on anymore leniency. Simon was still crossing all of his fingers, but he had hope that the justice system would finally step up.

He was also grateful to Sal, who noticed Simon kept looking behind him at the ceremony and, after about ten minutes of waiting for the cops to show up, had told him to go back to the wedding and make sure Leilani was okay.

And she was. Which made him happier than he could say.

Eventually, the cheering settled down and then Frenchie was directing everyone toward the reception pavilion. People did indeed file out, talking amongst themselves, but Simon only had eyes for Leilani.

She looked tired but relieved, flashing him a grin as they walked to the reception area. She didn't say anything about what had just happened, so Simon assumed that she wasn't ready to discuss it. Which was fine with him. They could dissect it all later. For the moment he just wanted to look at her and enjoy his brother's reception.

Because *goodness* was she something to look at. Simon had always thought that she was beautiful—but seeing her dressed in a peachy sort of coral, her long hair loose and flowing down her back, well, he just hadn't been prepared for it. Every time he looked at her, he felt like he saw something new and wonderful. She was so far out of his league that it wasn't even funny.

She was so distracting that he almost forgot what they were doing, only recalling that they were supposed to be finding their reserved seats at one of the family tables while they waited for the wedding photos. Gripping Leilani's hand, he gently guided her until he found their spots at a table to the left of the wedding table, along with Sal and Nova, then two other friends of Frenchie's. At the other table were Sterling and Elizabeth, Teddy and Silas, then Samuel and Virginia. Simon was excited to see his eldest brother. It felt like it had been *ages*.

But that could wait until after the speeches and all that, which would probably be soon. Although the wedding party had already taken pictures, there was a video playing that Solomon put together talking about his and Frenchie's story and the charities they were working with. Cute moments of them at the beach, Frenchie laughing after being hit in the face with a beachball. A video of her painting and Solomon distracting her with different things until she playfully smeared blue across his nose. Selfies of them in France, Frenchie looking up at the Eiffel tower in wonder while Solomon gazed in open admiration at her.

Simon watched all of it while appetizers were being passed around by the wait staff so folks wouldn't grow too hungry while waiting for the wedding party. Every moment he saw that flashed across the screen hanging down from the ceiling was magical. And he couldn't help but imagine having similar ones with Leilani.

Her spread out in the sand, looking up at him with her eyes shaded and scolding him to put on sunscreen. Them making spam musubi together and her laughing when he accidentally messed up his third roll. Him holding her, looking out at the night sky as they sat on the dock.

Was he getting ahead of himself? Absolutely. But he couldn't help it. Whenever he looked at Leilani, he just wanted *so much* for her.

He also wanted to be her man.

She must have noticed him staring because she sent him a dreamy sort of grin.

"Thank you," she murmured, a blush on her cheeks.

Simon leaned in under the pretense of needing to hear her, but really it was just to be closer to her. "For what?"

"Everything," she said softly.

Something about her tone made his face turn back to hers, and he hadn't realized just how close he'd leaned in. She was barely a breath away, her dark coral lips and kohl-lined eyes drawing his attention.

"It was all you, Leilani," he whispered back. "It's always been you."

It was beautiful watching color rise up her cheeks and into her face. Her eyes flicked away from him, only returning when one of the servers offered up some mini-crab cakes and shrimp cocktail. Simon knew Leilani loved seafood, so he grabbed two of each for them to munch on while they waited.

Like he expected, the wedding party didn't take long. Apparently Solomon and Frenchie had already written out and sent their photographer their "must-have" photos, so there wasn't any time lost shuffling about or thinking who to put where. Simon had never thought of doing that himself, but he took note in case he was ever the one getting married.

Funny, before Leilani, he had never thought beyond a short date or company for when traveling through a city. That seemed so shallow now, not enough to sustain him. Like he'd been living on sugar and junk food for his soul and now he craved something wholesome. Something nourishing.

Simon found himself grinning as Solomon and Frenchie welcomed them both to the reception. How they explained to guests that it was a dry event without any alcohol and thanked everyone for understanding that they'd deferred wedding presents in favor of donations to their chosen charities or gifts to the local community center. It was sweet, especially when they kept getting distracted by each other and leaning over to gently kiss each other. On the cheek. On the forehead. On the lips. It was like being too far from each other was physically painful for them.

Then it was time for the speeches. It was Silas who gave the best man speech and Tawny who gave the maid of honor speech, both talking about how they watched their respective friend or brother grow and learn to trust another human being.

His heart was achy in a good way when they finished, and of course there was applause all around. Thankfully Frenchie and Solomon had also said that while they were very happy to be man and wife, they wouldn't be kissing every time someone hit a fork against their glass, so at least there wasn't a high pitched chorus of glassy clangs after every sentence. Simon had been to a couple of weddings where one or two audience members always got real clang-happy and wouldn't let the couple get a word in edgewise.

But then one set of clapping went on too long, and heads started to swivel to the table right in front of the bridal party.

Of course, it was Dad. Mr. Miller himself, clapping in such a sarcastic way that it was practically dripping all over the table.

He was drunk. How did he get drunk at a dry wedding?

"Bravo, bravo. Everyone happy, everyone smiling, but the story sure is polished up here, isn't it?" He stood, despite Mom grabbing at his arm and hissing at him to sit. "As if you couldn't tell by that outburst that happened earlier, this is what my family has been going through since my sons have decided to invite these women into our home. And Francesca was the start of it.

"Imagine your son, the one you rely on, suddenly starts shirking his duties, starts arguing with me, starts proposing ideas counter to everything we'd built our family business up to be together. And then, you look into who's taking up all his time and find out that a criminal from another state has somehow caught your heir up."

Another murmur from the audience. Leilani was sitting straight up, her eyes darting from Mr. Miller to the wedding table, clearly uncertain what to do. Simon also didn't know what to say. That was his *father*, but also that was his *brother*. What was the protocol?

"Yeah, that's right. A *criminal*. Notice how none of them mentioned that. But that's how they get you, you know. These gold diggers. Cause let's be honest, that's what they are. We can all dance around it as much as we want, but we all know it. These women—"

Suddenly Mrs. Miller was on her feet, gripping her husband's arm and yanking him away from the table.

Not a single word was said as she dragged him out, aside from Mr. Miller protesting that he needed to finish his speech. Most people were staring after them, the wedding party silent.

Nearly a full minute passed because Frenchie cleared her throat again. "Well, nobody can ever say that this was a boring wedding."

Uneasy laughter, and then they were shakily moving forward. Simon got the feeling that maybe Leilani was relieved that drama that didn't involve her was the most recent thing that happened. She didn't say it, of course, but she did seem more relaxed.

Finally, without any more bumps, hiccups, or interruptions, it was time for the actual meal. Each person had the plate that they'd requested on their RSVP, with more available for request if folks were particularly hungry. Which would at least be Sal. Simon's brother was always going on about something called "marcos" or "macros" or something.

And then, after the meal was done, came the first dance. It was between Solomon and Frenchie, and if anyone thought it was odd that there was no dance between the bride and her father, everyone had the good sense not to say so. Instead they all got to watch as Solomon wrapped his arms around the love of his life and the two began to slowly dance together to a Spanish song that Simon didn't understand, but he didn't need to speak the language to hear the love in it.

A sniffle from Leilani towards the end drew his attention, and he looked away from the couple to see she was dabbing at the corner of her eye with a napkin.

"It's really sweet," she murmured, clearly embarrassed when she realized that he was looking at her. "And I guess maybe I'm a little emotional today."

"I mean, it's not like you don't have a reason to be. A lot has happened today."

"Yeah. It has." She let out a long breath. "I'm trying to believe that he's actually gone, which is hard considering what happened the last time."

Simon nodded. "Yeah, I can't blame you. But the PI assured

me that there's almost no chance of bail and with all these witnesses, the case is basically foolproof."

"I've got all my fingers crossed."

He nodded and turned his attention back to his brother. *Man*, Solomon looked so happy. While he wasn't the most outgoing of the brothers, Solomon had always been kind. Simon had heard horror stories about older siblings who bullied and fought their younger ones, but none of his older brothers had ever been like that. So, it was good to see him finally getting what he deserved, which was a beautiful wife who he clearly loved to the moon and back.

Simon thought about Leilani, because of course he did. He wasn't to Solomon's level, of course. He had so much to learn about her, so much more to listen to and talk about. But he could see the potential of it in the air, and he *wanted* that. He wanted that more than he'd ever wanted anything or anyone in his whole life.

The couple's song ended and there was more clapping and plenty of crying from several attendees. Then the dance floor was open to everybody, starting with one of those cheesy group dances that everyone always joked about white people loving.

The thing was... Simon *really* did love them. Even if they were silly.

"Do you wanna dance?" Leilani asked him, her eyes going down to his tapping foot.

When had that happened? He didn't recall telling his foot to move.

"Naw, it's alright," he said, feeling his cheeks color slightly. A small part of him was embarrassed at the idea of Leilani seeing him all goofy and unchecked. He wanted to impress her, to be her tall and strong cowboy, and dancing in a line while clapping and hopping didn't seem the best way to do it.

"You sure?" Leilani said, offering her hand. "Because I love all these cheesy dances. Especially when the kids can play along too." She pointed over her shoulder where some of the youngest of attendees were indeed cutting a rug with their parents, and it looked like even a couple of grandparents.

"Well…" That small embarrassed part gave one last push, but it wasn't enough to defeat the majority of him that would never pass up an opportunity to dance with Leilani. "If you insist."

"I think I do."

Then they were up and walking over to the dance floor, jumping in just as the song ordered them to slide to the left.

And it *was* silly, but that was the point of it. It was silly and fun and absolutely as far from serious as they could get. Which was what they desperately needed after so much fear, anger, and everything else that had come in a Kai-shaped package.

After the silly song came another one that *everyone* knew, then a line dance. Simon was a bit breathless from laughter and fun, sure that he hadn't had such a great time since he first started college.

But then a slow song started—one of those romantic ones where people coupled up and rocked gently across the dance floor together. He looked to Leilani uncertainly only to see that she was gazing at him with plenty of trepidation on her own.

Like something out of the movies he used to watch with his mom back in the day, he extended his hand to her. "May I have this dance?"

"We're already dancing," she whispered, and he watched the way the column of her throat bobbed. "We've been dancing around each other this whole time."

That really was the truth, wasn't it? The two of them interacted first at that diner, then did their best to avoid each other for the two months after that until Kai had showed up and forced them together. What would have happened if he'd never shown up? Would Simon have kept on avoiding her, trying to give her space while desperately wishing he could close that gap between them? Would she go on thinking of him as that guy she turned down?

Maybe. But he was glad they weren't in that timeline at all.

"Then maybe we should dance together."

She almost seemed to glow as a slow smile spread across her face. "Yeah. Maybe we should."

And then her hand was in his, soft and cool and wonderful, as her body drew into his. His hands went to her waist, resting in the cushiony nip in there before her hips flared out. The fabric was smooth, almost slippery under his hands, and the pads of his fingers dragged against it.

One sensation after another, all of them heady and important, building on top of each other until it felt like they were in a dreamworld, just the two of them swaying to the music.

And he felt centered, whole, and meant to be exactly where he was. There was no itch in his feet to go. There was no desire to be somewhere else, anywhere else. There was just... peace.

Peace, and a bittersweet sort of longing for the woman who was so soft and brave in his arms.

"Simon?"

Her voice almost startled him—he hadn't realized he'd closed his eyes—and he opened them again to look down at her. He didn't know how, but it was like he'd forgotten how breathtaking she was already.

"Yeah?"

"That first day you met me, why did you ask me out?"

Oh. *That.*

He didn't really want to say, but he also didn't want to ever withhold anything from Leilani, so he cleared his throat and tried to answer as honestly as he could. "It was a lot of things, really. First of all, you're beautiful, but you know that."

"Do I?" she said, those perfect lips of hers curling into a wry smile, her gray eyes sparkling at him in the romantic lights that Frenchie had ordered from a small business online. Apparently bought them out of their whole stock too.

"It would literally be impossible for you not to."

"It's nice hearing you say it."

"Is it?"

"Mmhmm." She leaned her head against his shoulder and the vibration of her voice wrapped around his heart, making the beat of it waver. She so viscerally affected him and she wasn't even trying. It was insane. "What else?"

"Well, you were clever. And you surprised me."

"Surprised you?"

"Yeah, I guess you can say I'm used to being able to predict people. After going to college and earning several degrees then traveling around the world, I guess you could say that I thought I knew everything about everyone. But then you sauntered up to me, and suddenly I was faced with someone who could keep up. Someone who was funny and could banter with me. And..." he licked his lips, not sure if he should keep going. "You made me feel seen."

"Seen?"

He nodded. "It's not like I'm invisible. I'm aware enough to know plenty of people find me attractive. But that's what they see first. And if they know my family, they see the money and the prestige. But you didn't seem to care about my looks and you certainly didn't seem to know who I was, so it was like I was actually being judged on my personality. My being."

"All that, and all I did was recommend you a burger and a monster pancake."

"I mean, to be fair, it was a *really* good pancake."

"I told you so."

The song ended, but it drifted into another one in... Italian, he thought. It was one his Aunt Annie up north used to sing when he and his brothers visited back when they were very little. Not to them, of course. But she would sing it to her husband sometimes while they rocked together on the porch, with the entire brood of boys playing out in their massive yard.

And so they stayed in each other's arms, swaying and stepping to the beat.

"Leilani?"

"Yeah?"

"I'm pretty sure I know the answer, but why did you say no?"

"I'm sure you've already figured it out, but I haven't dated anyone since Kai. I was too scared and too off-put by the idea. Like, I know that statistically speaking, all men can't be like him, but it's too terrifying to also know that I can't tell which men *are* like him without making myself vulnerable.

"It was hard to even want to date, considering that I always had this fear he would find me. It seemed impossible, stressful, and awful. Not to mention a handsome man asking me out at work sure did remind me of Kai doing the same back before I knew any better."

So, it was all of the reasons he thought it was. That was a relief in a way.

"Why do you ask?" she continued.

"Because I wanted to make sure it wasn't because you didn't like my personality or because you thought I looked like a troll."

She laughed at that, full and lush and oh so wonderful. "No, hardly. You're funny and you're nothing like a troll. It was all because of Kai. And because I needed to get to know you."

"And what's your judgment now that you've gotten to know me?"

She stammered for a moment and he felt her heart thunder against his chest. "That maybe I wouldn't mind getting to know you a little more. You know, once things calm down."

"Is that so?"

She nodded and then she was looking at him again, eyes so open and full of trust that he wasn't quite sure that he deserved. "Yeah. That's absolutely so. I've spent so many years being afraid and living a sort of half-life, that I want to do all the things I told myself I never could. I want to find out who twenty-something Leilani is."

Simon's heart soared with that, filling him with a kind of contentment he couldn't describe. Because no matter what happened between him and Leilani, she was finally free. And even if it was her strength that had allowed his plan to work, he could take pride in the fact that he had helped her.

"I'd like to find out who she is too."

"I guess you're stuck hanging out with me then."

"I'd like that."

Another pause, but then the tension faded from her limbs and she leaned into him even further. "I'd like that too."

He knew he probably shouldn't, that he was being greedy and asking too much, but then his mouth was off and doing its own thing again. "Do you think—once things calm down—I might have a second chance to ask you about those dinner plans?"

He didn't want to push her boundaries in any way, shape, or form. Not after everything she'd been through. But with how she was looking at him, how she was *talking* to him, he couldn't help but wonder if things had changed.

If not, he would accept it. He wouldn't fight it. And he would be the best friend and protector she ever had. But he hoped, deep within his heart, that maybe she saw him differently than the monster she'd escaped from.

"You know what, Simon?" Her lips curled in that perfect, snarky way of hers. "That sounds like a good plan."

He grinned too, his heart feeling like it could launch out of his chest, and abruptly there was movement. Leilani pushed herself up on her toes, her hands gripping him for balance, and her lips ever so gently brushed against his.

It was barely there, and over in a moment, but it was like his entire body went offline. He blinked several times, trying to get his brain to come back to the present, and when he did, Leilani was blushing vibrantly in his arms.

"Something wrong?" he managed to ask although his tongue felt heavy in his mouth and he very much wanted to kiss her again. But deeper, longer, in a way that would let him learn what made her sigh and melt into him like there was nothing outside of them in the entire world.

"No, not at all. Just thinking that you're only the second person I've ever kissed."

Oh.

"Well, if you ever need a little more practice to make sure you're not rusty, I'd be happy to oblige you."

She laughed, shaking her head. "I'll let you know."

"Please do."

They sank back into silence, just listening to the music and enjoying the thrum of each other's bodies. The song ended too soon, the same as the song before it, and another group song came up.

"Let's have a sit," Leilani said, face flushed. "Give our feet a break."

Simon was about to remark that his feet were fine, but then he realized that Leilani was wearing heels. It was no doubt best to defer to her judgment on the matter.

"Yeah, let's."

The rest of the reception went off without a hitch, although Simon didn't get to spend as much of it with just him and Leilani as he would have liked. His brothers all wanted to talk to him, then he wanted to congratulate the newlyweds, and of course all of the Millers wanted to do the electric slide.

There was also the matter of catching up with his cousins. A majority of them were missing after the shenanigans from Simon's graduation dinner, but there were several still there. Bradley and Keiko, for one. Simon couldn't be sure, but he was fairly certain that the woman's stomach was slightly rounded. Or at least more rounded than the few times he'd seen her at his aunt and uncle's place. The thought of Bradley Miller, the family's problem child, settling down to be a father was something else, alright.

But even the best of events had to come to an end, and Simon found himself driving Leilani home somewhere just before eleven p.m. They arrived at the mansion, exhausted, but he still made sure to walk her to her bedroom door on his arm.

Of course, a very un-subtle throat clearing from Auntie Kini told them that they weren't alone. Not that anything would have happened, of course. Leilani's confession that he was only her second kiss made him pretty certain that she was inexperienced in other ways. Or worse, her only experience was with Kai. If Simon was honest with himself, he'd strayed from the path plenty of times during his first year in college, and once or twice when he was abroad.

But he didn't want any of that now. He just wanted to be by Leilani's side in whatever capacity she needed.

"Goodnight, Simon. Thank you. For everything."

"Goodnight, Leilani," he said, bending down to place the gentlest of kisses against her forehead. "Sweet dreams."

"You know what? I think for once they will be."

19

———

Simon

Simon had been planning another night out with his friends when he got a text from his mom asking him to come to Dad's study. Unusual, and concern immediately perked up in him.

He treaded toward the center of the upper floor, meeting Silas and Sal as they came up the stairs. Together, the three of them filed into the study to find Sterling and Solomon there too. All of the McLintoc Miller brothers—minus Samuel, plus their parents. That was probably a first since Simon's graduation dinner.

"Is everything okay?" Simon asked slowly. Horrible ideas flashed through his mind from cancer to Alzheimer's to stroke. But both of his parents looked well enough.

"I'll just get this started," Mom said, clearing her throat. "I wanted to let all of you know that Dad and I have agreed to attend a counseling program together."

"Counseling? What kind of counseling?" That was Silas, who looked more confused than anything.

"Marriage, faith, and family," she answered honestly. "There need to be some serious changes in order to improve the health of our marriage and the family. Somewhere along the way, we've gotten derailed, and we've become enemies more than blood. That's not the family I've always dreamed of, so we're doing something to change that."

Simon looked to Mr. Miller, trying to guess what he was thinking. But the man was just sitting there stoically beside her, his face frozen.

But then... Simon looked into his eyes, and he saw pain there. He saw a man who looked like he was lost at sea without an oar.

Simon knew that feeling.

"Also, your dad is voluntarily resigning from his position at the head of his company. We thought it would be best since we will be going away to our counseling retreat for about a month, and then we're going to travel to all the places we promised ourselves to go before returning to rebuild the trust that's been broken here."

She looked at Solomon. "Both you and Samuel will be running the company as Co-Presidents should you accept the position while the rest of you will have equal Vice President positions if you want. But you are all more than welcome to stay in your current positions, if you should so desire."

"Wait," Solomon said, standing ramrod straight. "Is this real? Are you guys serious about this?"

"We are," Mom said, nodding resolutely. "Right, McLintoc?"

"Your mother is correct," McLintoc Miller said somewhat hollowly.

That seemed to be the catalyst because suddenly everyone was hugging each other and wishing each other well and expressing amazement. But Simon wasn't ready to embrace it out yet. His dad was one of the most stubborn people he knew, and he had a hard time believing that the man was just willing to get up and abandon the thing he'd sacrificed the relationship with all of his children to build.

Quietly, he took a knee so he could meet his dad eye to eye. He saw some of his own features in the man's face, and it was so easy to see how he could follow right in his dad's footsteps.

"Is this what you really want?" he asked, voice low. He wanted honesty. He wanted his dad to be candid with him in a way he hadn't been since they were very young.

"I'm... it's not what I would have chosen, and I'm not exactly happy about it," the man answered after a long pause, his eyes darting around the room to where his other sons were hugging Mom, their backs turned to him. "But the idea of gaining all the wealth in the world doesn't come close to being worth it if my whole life is just going to be fighting with my sons and losing the love of my life." There was a raw, open sort of pain that Simon didn't think he'd ever seen on his dad before. "I know how I may seem, but I can't live without her, Simon. She's my everything. And even though I don't always act like it, so are you boys."

His dad let out a soft sound, which was perhaps the closest to a sob that he would ever allow himself. "I wondered sometimes, how I ever got to this place. Such an awful, awful place." He let out a long breath, and Simon felt his heart ache with him. "Don't be like me, son. Because the only time I ever feel much happiness is when your mother looks at me with pride, and she hasn't done that in what feels like ages."

"I won't, Dad. But it's not too late to change. It never is."

Mr. Miller nodded, looking so utterly exhausted. "Let's hope you're right, son. Let's hope you're right."

20

Leilani

To say that life calmed down after the wedding wasn't exactly accurate. Solomon and Frenchie went off on their honeymoon while Mrs. and Mr. Miller were going on some sort of... relationship trip? Leilani wasn't exactly clear on the details, but from what she understood, it was going to be real good for them.

As for herself, she had to make several trips into the city for the Kai situation as well as set a whole list of court-appointed dates into her calendar, as well as figure out what her new normal was.

And one of those things about her new normal was not having to live at the Miller ranch.

She loved it there, she did. But it also wasn't her home. It was very much the Miller's house and she was a guest there. A guest of a son who was considering moving back because something about being a co-President with Solomon?

Of course, they still needed to wait to make sure Kai didn't pull any shenanigans again. But after a month and a half with him safely behind bars, she and Auntie Kini started making plans. The older woman went back to her home while at the two-month mark, Leilani moved into a nice, one-bedroom apartment on the edge of the city just like she had planned to before her ex came and derailed everything.

Then there was unpacking, buying décor that she could actually afford for once, and before she knew it, summer was over and they were in the middle of fall. She didn't know how time had gotten so far away from them, but it was exactly at the three-month mark that Simon had asked her to that dinner she'd promised him.

And of course, she'd agreed. In the three months that had passed since the wedding, Simon had been a constant friend and source of comfort for her. He listened to her, he helped her be brave when she was so used to thinking she could never do something. He was quickly becoming her closest confidant. Closer than Nova even— because the woman was taking classes again thanks to Sal and didn't have nearly as much time.

But it was more than just friendship, if she was up front with herself. The more time she spent with Simon, the more her face would flush when she saw him, and her heart would skip. Sometimes, when they were doing something innocuous like making snacks or he was teaching her to ride a horse, her mind would flash back to one of those intense moments between them, like with the spam musubi or s'more or at the wedding reception. In fact, a lot of their moments seemed to revolve around food, and Leilani subconsciously wondered if that was why she kept trying to feed the man.

But it was finally his turn to feed her, and she found herself fidgeting nervously as she waited in her new apartment for him to pick her up.

So much could go wrong. He could be a wolf in disguise. She could say or do something that made him think she was gross. Or annoying. He could do something that was gross or annoying. There were so many negatives, she didn't understand why anyone would go through with dating at all.

But then she thought of the electricity that flooded her when she'd just barely kissed Simon. She thought about the curl of his lips when she said something especially witty. And she thought of the way that he looked at her sometimes when he thought she wouldn't notice, then dating made plenty of sense.

She rode that seesaw of emotion until he texted her that he was there, and she headed to her door.

Leilani had expected him to be pulled up to the front of the apartment building, but she hadn't anticipated him to be standing right there at the locked door, a bouquet of flowers in his hands.

These ones were all hibiscus, with baby's breath peeping out between the brilliant petals.

"Hey there," he said, offering her his arm. "You look amazing."

Leilani looked down at her ensemble that Teddy had helped her put together. It was a simple, blue gingham top with a Peter Pan collar while she wore a flared circle skirt at the bottom. Simon had asked her to wear something that she was comfortable moving around in, so she had bicycle shorts on underneath and comfortable flats.

"Oh, this ol' thang?" she said, putting on an exaggerated accent and batting her eyes at him. He looked nice too, with a dark green button-up shirt and hardy looking blue jeans. "Are those actual cowboy boots?"

"Well, I do live on a ranch, you know."

"Oh, I know. I just... huh. They look good on you."

"Thanks."

It shouldn't have been possible for a single word to make her heart miss a beat, but it did, and the next thing she knew, she was sliding into his truck and they were headed off into the southern part of the city.

"I'm not familiar with this area," she remarked as they drove along.

"Did you ever take much time to explore the city?"

"...no. I suppose not. Too much of a chance of being seen."

Simon didn't laugh at her or tell her she was paranoid. He just nodded and went into some of the places he wanted to show her. He was so impossibly sweet. Did he even know?

No, probably not.

They arrived at a large, well-lit bar. As soon as they entered, Leilani realized what was going on.

"Oh my gosh, you've brought me line dancing?" she asked, a startled laugh bubbling out of her.

"Yeah, that's alright... right?"

Leilani let another giddy laugh pass her lips. "I've always wanted to try this. How did you know?"

"Well, at the wedding, I remember you asking how everyone knew the same moves, and I figured maybe you wanted to learn."

He noticed that? She hadn't even remembered. Throwing her arms around him, she hugged him tightly. "You're brilliant, you know that? Brilliant."

"I mean... I might have suspected, but it sure does sound nice when you say it."

"Then I'll keep saying it."

Leilani grabbed his hand and went right onto the dance floor and let both him and the speaker help her along. She wasn't very good, but that didn't matter. She loved the music and the laughter, and everyone all moving together. It felt like she was a part of something, like she belonged instead of being some outsider who was just trying to exist until their hunter found them again.

It really was a whole new life, and she owed it all to Simon.

After fifteen minutes she was breathless and sweaty, so they took a break to drink water and snack on peanuts then were back on the dance floor. Leilani could have stayed there until her feet fell off, but after two very fun and exhausting hours, Simon was escorting her back out.

"Isn't it a little early to call it a night?" she asked as he opened the truck door for her and helped her in. She didn't need the help, of course, but that didn't mean she didn't like it.

"Who said we were calling it a night?" he replied blithely before going around to his side of the vehicle.

Despite his coyness, she noticed that they did head back toward the estate. She was bummed that they were going home before she remembered that she didn't live at the Miller mansion anymore, practically face-palming over her own thoughts.

It turned out that they weren't going to the estate either. Instead they took an earlier exit and drove until they pulled off at what she recognized as a hiking trail.

She felt slightly nervous considering what had happened the last time that she was on a "camping trip," but those nerves settled when Simon came around and took her hand.

"It's just beyond those trees. I promise. Oh!" He reached past her into the glove compartment and grabbed a small canvas bag.

The movement drew their bodies oh so close together, and Leilani felt her breath crash.

He was so *warm* and so solid against her, sturdy. Assuring. She wondered what he would do if she pressed herself to him like she had at the wedding, where they'd swayed around in each other's arms in what felt like an entirely different world.

But she stayed still, her heart beating like a timpani drum. But then Simon reached into the bag and handed her a can of bug spray.

"You might want to put this on."

Huh, well citronella wasn't exactly a romantic scent, but bug bites were definitely a mood killer, so she went about spraying herself down, then Simon followed suit.

"Ready?"

"For what?"

There was that curl to his lips again. Goodness, she felt like she could fall right into that. "You'll see."

Before she could tell him that wasn't fair, her hand was in his and he was leading her to the line of trees with the light of his phone.

It was a little nerve-racking, but almost as soon as they were under the branches, they were out from them, looking at a grassy plateau that looked over a mini-valley.

"What's this?" she asked, looking around. He didn't have a picnic basket or a blanket with him, so it seemed unlikely that it was some romantic dinner under the stars.

"Hold on," Simon said, looking past her and pulling something from the bag.

She was surprised to see a sparkler, which he stuck in the

ground and lit. It went up easily, sparkling as its name implied. She began to wonder if it was some sort of bizarre mainland tradition that she wasn't familiar with when suddenly, little dots of yellow light began to illuminate all around her.

One by one, like tiny stars, they illuminated in waves, flickering and winking at her. It was magic, pure and simple, and she found herself giggling in sheer amazement again.

"W-what is this?" she asked, sounding breathless even to herself.

"They're fireflies. Also known as lightning bugs," Simon answered, turning and grinning at her.

Right, she knew about those, she'd just never *seen* them before. They were like fairies, popping in and out of her sight all around her.

"I read that they're not native to the islands, so I figured you've never been able to see them like this."

"I've seen pictures and on TV. But in person, it's just so..." She shook her head. She didn't have the right words for it.

"If you like *this*, just wait a minute."

Before she could ask him what he meant, he walked forward and lit another sparkler further ahead. Sure enough, the entire field began to light up, flowing and rippling, gentle waves across the burgundy velvet of the night.

"Texas alone has thirty-six different species of fireflies, and look, I think they're all here to say hi to you."

They weren't, of course, but the sincerity in his voice made Leilani believe it. Her throat grew tight and she felt tears prick at the corners of her eyes. Holding her hand out, one of the beautiful little bugs landed on her, glowing brightly, before taking off again.

They were *so beautiful*, full of the magic and beauty that

God had managed to pack into the world. The beauty of it was almost too much and Leilani had to focus on her breathing.

"Are you tired of dancing?" Simon asked gently.

The words were out of her mouth before she even thought them through. "I don't know if I can ever get tired of dancing with you."

"I'm mighty pleased to hear that." Gently, he brought her to him, and their bodies aligned just like they had at the wedding three months earlier. "I can assure you, the feeling's mutual."

He picked a song from his phone, the gentle notes only slightly tinny through the speakers, and then they were floating through the field, swirling and whirling with the fireflies dancing in kind.

"You look like a beautiful, mystical queen, and I'm some foolish mortal who's stumbled into your court," he whispered after a long time of them moving together, lost in the world they created, just the two of them.

"A Cowboy in the Fairy Court, huh? I'd read that."

"Oh, would you?"

"Definitely. It'd be a number one best seller, I'm sure."

He chuckled lightly and then his grip on her tightened ever so slightly. He was nervous. "Leilani, I have a bit of a confession to make..."

Uh... was that good or bad? Swallowing, she lifted her face to look at him. "That sounds rather dire."

"Does it? I guess it could be. But, uh, I suppose..."

"It's okay, Simon, say what you need to."

"Alright. I... I'm sure you've put it together, but I've been told I need to say it outright. I understand that you've been through a whole lot, and that you may need to move slow—and there might be some things that you'll never want to do at all— but I want us to be together, Leilani."

"You're here with me right now," she whispered, her heart pounding in her chest.

He gave her one of those *looks* that he gave her when she was being smart-mouthed. But unlike Kai, he enjoyed her snarkiness. "You know what I mean."

"I need you to say it, Simon. I need you to speak the words."

He took a deep, shuddering breath. "Leilani Cunningham, I would very much like the chance to court you officially, because I'm pretty certain I'm in love with you."

Whoa.

There it was, existing in the real world, words that were uttered and couldn't be taken back.

And Leilani felt them down to her feet, making her toes curl in her flats and her heart flip over. He loved her, he *loved* her, and it was that real, sparking, protective love that wanted to see her do well. Not the viciously vindictive love that Kai had. Not the desire to own or control her. Some part of her knew that she could turn Simon down and—although he would be crushed—he would take her home without complaint. Would still be her friend.

"Okay," she said.

"Okay?"

"Yeah. Okay. Because I think I might be in love with you too."

She felt the ripple that went through him, somewhere between relief and excitement. "I understand if you need time."

"Oh, I do," she said. "I'm still figuring so much out. I'm figuring out how to say no and how to trust. I'm learning what it's like to just be able to do something because I want to. But I want to learn those things with you. Because I trust you. With all that I have."

His hold around her tightened again, but it was comforting,

not entrapping. "Thank you," he whispered into the top of her head.

"Thank *you*," she said. "I never would have a chance at this without you."

"I don't think you understand all that you've done for me, Leilani. And I don't know if I can put it into words."

"Well," she said, smiling up at him once more. "You have plenty of time to figure it out. For right now, how about one of those kissing lessons you mentioned earlier?"

She could see the fireflies reflected in his eyes as he gazed down at her. "I can do that."

And it was in the moonlight that shone down that Simon pressed his lips to hers in another kiss. Gentle, always so gentle, and full of promises that she would never have to fear him like she feared Kai.

Leilani had never felt so safe.

LEILANI'S EPILOGUE

"And this is my boyfriend, Simon."

"Why do you all have 's' names?" her little cousin, Lito, asked, his head curiously to the side. "And why are you so red?"

Simon chuckled and knelt down to look the little man in the face. "Well, I might have forgotten to put sunscreen on right after getting off the plane, and apparently your sun here is a lot stronger than our sun back home. As for my name, it's a family thing."

"It's 'cause we're so close to the elevator," her cousin responded.

"You mean the equator," Leilani corrected gently. "And what did Auntie Kailani tell you about talking about people's looks?"

The boy looked like he was thinking for a moment. "If it's not somfin' somebody can fix in one minute, don't mention it."

"There you go."

"Okies, sorry, mister. But if you need aloe, Momma's got lots in the fridge inside."

"Maybe later, Lito. I've already put some medicine and some sunscreen on him."

"Okie dokie, artichokies!" He ran off to join the other children playing.

Leilani gave Simon a little squeeze.

"You're doing great," she assured, patting his back.

"Other than being lectured about proper sun safety by an eight-year-old," he remarked with a grin. "Smart kid."

"We're all taught how to protect ourselves from a pretty young age. There's no ethnic majority here on the islands, so we make sure pale folks are just as protected as us with more melanin."

"Wait, there's no ethnic majority here?"

"Nope. Thirty percent people of Asian descent, thirty percent Caucasian and about, uh, twenty-five percent being native Hawaiian or part Native."

Simon's eyebrows went up at that. "Only twenty-five percent of your homeland actually is Native?"

She could see him trying to do the math in his head and just tugged his hand. "Come on, that's a conversation for a different day. Let me introduce you to more folks. I'm pretty sure Sal is being used as a jungle gym by the toddlers."

"Finally, a reason for him to have all those muscles," Simon remarked dryly before following her.

But Leilani was having the time of her life. It had been a year and a half since she and Simon had started dating, and they'd both come so far. But without a doubt, everything was so much *better.*

For one, Kai was well and truly dealt with. He'd been returned back to Hawaii and was sitting in a cell and would be for several years. There was no getting out on bail and very unlikely that he would get out on good behavior. It was safe for her to do whatever she wanted and explore life with Simon.

She even had started college! Something that she'd always thought was out of her grasp. Yet she was already a full semester down and rocking it as the second recipient of the Salvatore Miller Scholarship Fund. Despite her knack with animals, she'd always had a far-off dream of getting into engineering and had gotten into a pretty ambitious program.

In fact, that was the whole reason that they were in Hawaii, celebrating her first successful semester. Mrs. and Mr. Miller were there, as well as Sal, Nova, Teddy, and Silas. The patriarch was doing much better and there seemed to be peace in the house, although there were still the occasional clashes.

Leilani still wasn't a fan of his, but she believed Simon when he said his dad wanted to change. So, she gave him the space and the chance to do so and hoped that he would do exactly as he promised.

Her family was thrilled to have her back for a visit, of course, even if they weren't very happy that she was making her home in Texas. They'd arranged a big ol' luau, and she was having a great time introducing the Miller clan to her loved ones.

They were doing well, except for Simon's sunscreen incident, and everyone was getting along.

It was a dream. A wonderful dream that she never would have dared to have a year and a half earlier. And with every new event, every new comment, she wanted to pinch herself to believe that it was real.

"So," her Auntie Kailani said as Mom placed spam musubi on both her and Simon's plate. It was no secret that he'd grown to love the snack since he and Leilani started dating, and her mom was thrilled to pieces. "Have you had *poi* yet?"

"No," Simon said, looking around. "But is this everyone that's supposed to be here?"

"Uh, yeah, I think so," her Uncle Bennie said, standing up. "It was Sayong and Maichi who were the last ones to show up, right?"

"Right."

"Okay then."

Suddenly Simon was standing, clearing his throat. "Excuse me, uh, Leilani's *ohana,* if I could have your attention."

What was he doing? Why was he talking like that?

Leilani stared as he stepped over the bench that they were on, then knelt down on one knee in front of her, pulling a box from his pocket.

"Leilani Kamea Cunningham, you are the single most amazing woman that I have ever met, and I want to spend the rest of my life with you. I am a better man with a bigger world because of you, and I'm so excited to see what we can do together in the future.

"If you would want to be by my side, I could think of no greater honor than you agreeing to be my bride. So, Leilani, will you marry me?"

Her whole body thrummed, and her heart practically leapt out of her throat and it was ever so wonderful. "Yes!" she cried. "Yes, yes, *absolutely* yes!"

She threw her arms around him and he picked her up, holding her as they laughed and cried and otherwise made a mess of themselves. He kissed her and she kissed him back, surrounded by the cheers of her family.

When they finally parted, Leilani felt a gentle tug on her dress.

"Yes, Mimi?" she asked her youngest sister, who was standing there looking up at her.

"Can I be your flower girl?"

"Of course," Leilani answered with a laugh, sweeping the girl up in her arms. "You absolutely can."

SIMON'S EPILOGUE

Time passed ever so quickly, and every single day of it was a blessing. Events tumbled one right after another, and Simon was more present for them than he'd ever been before.

Elizabeth and Sterling's winter wedding went off without a hitch, another notch to draw the family closer together.

Leilani entered her second year of school and was still rocking it, calling him each day to tell him about what she learned and how amazing it was. Those were some of his favorite times, listening to her be so happy and excited. He remembered what a gift college had been for him, an oasis in the vast ocean that he was always lost in, and he was more than happy his family had been able to provide that for her.

Then his family traveled up north for Samuel's wedding. He and his bride were pulling double duty, living half of the year with Aunt Annie and Uncle Douglas and the other half down at the McLintoc Miller ranch helping Solomon reform things.

Unfortunately, Dad didn't come to that one, but he did send

a letter. It was going to take a long time, but Dad looked like he was at least trying to make up for things with his eldest son. He just had quite the path to travel.

Little by little, his family was healing. There were still fissures. Still issues. The cousins to the west were still leery of them and both Samuel and his wife were... cautious. Which was a shame because the blond woman was hilarious and steadfast, telling them with no qualms that anyone who insulted her loving husband would be personally laid out by her. And judging by her biceps, Simon believed her. Of course, Missy would always nod along in agreement, looking as sure and as confident as ever.

And naturally, once those two met Leilani, they became fast friends, and his fiancée grew interested in the self-defense that the women taught. Simon was worried at first—he hated the thought of her being hurt—but seeing how happy and confident she looked whenever she learned a new move to protect herself wiped away any doubts he'd had.

Life was good. Not perfect, but good, and improving every day. So when Simon woke up to another beautiful day, he got ready and headed out to work on the ranch, greeting his brothers he came across, greeting their wives or fiancées he came across, and of course saying hi to the animals that looked his way.

He found Leilani in the kid pen, because naturally, reading a textbook while petting the little mischief-makers with her other hand made her happy.

"Hey there," he said, carefully hopping over the fence and handing her a thermos of iced coffee. She almost always forgot it in the mornings when she visited on the weekends, so he didn't mind bringing it to her.

"Thank you," she murmured, taking a long drink. "So I've been thinking more about the house we're going to build."

"Uh-huh?"

As much as his family was healing, they didn't want to have their first years as newlyweds in the big manor. Sure, Solomon and Frenchie had chosen to live there, but it just wasn't the right fit for Simon and Leilani.

"And I'd like a garden. A *big* one."

"We can do that."

"Good."

She nodded and went back to her book, a latent grin on her face. Simon couldn't resist and bent down to give her a kiss on the cheek.

He should have known better, because one of the kids playfully headbutted the back of his knees, almost making him topple over. Leilani steadied him, however, and let out that melodic laugh he loved.

"Let's hope Frenchie's kid isn't as hard-headed as all the goats she's named."

"Yeah, I—" Simon's brain caught up to her words a moment later. "Wait, what?"

"Frenchie's kid." When he continued to stare at her, she finally looked up from her book. "What, you didn't notice that she's gotten hungrier, shorter-tempered, and takes a nap or two every day?"

"Um... no. I haven't paid enough attention to Frenchie's habits to know that."

"Oh. Well. I noticed." Leilani gave a shrug and bent to pick up her toppled notebook. "At least Elizabeth is around a month behind her so both babies won't come at the same time."

Simon's eyes went wider than he thought possible. "Did, uh, one of them tell you this?"

"What? No. I'm just real good at watching people. I first got curious when I noticed that Elizabeth's walk had completely changed. She had such an authoritative stride, you know, I could always recognize her steps across the floor. But now she's got almost this little waddle to her. It's cute.

"Then I noticed she stopped wearing pants with non-stretch waistlines and has been taking vitamins with every meal. And considering how little the feminine products in the work bathrooms have been used, it was easy enough to put two and two together."

"I... that's incredible. Are you sure?"

"Sure enough," Leilani said with one of those grins that never failed to dazzle him. But something in it wavered, and her expression grew serious. "Simon?"

"Uh-huh."

"Do you ever want kids?"

Oh.

Simon swallowed, taking a minute to order his thoughts. He'd promised Leilani to always be honest, and he had no intention of breaking that promise. "I never really thought of it, actually." But now that she'd mentioned it, his mind went off on its own, imagining what it would be like to have little ones racing around with Leilani's hair, nose, and spirit, but his eyes and maybe a few freckles. How they would have her laugh but his teeth, and how they would learn and grow and become their own adults with their own stories.

And suddenly, he liked the idea.

He liked that idea a whole lot.

He didn't think he said that last part out loud, but he must have, because Leilani was closing her book and standing on tiptoe to press a tender kiss to his lips.

"Well, you better help me plan our wedding then. The

sooner the ring is on here, the sooner we can work on whatever it was you just saw in your mind."

"Yes, *ma'am*," Simon said, offering his arm to her.

She took it, and together they walked inside. He was no longer listless, purposeless, or unmoored. He'd finally found his home.

Who knew that it was always right where he'd left it.

~

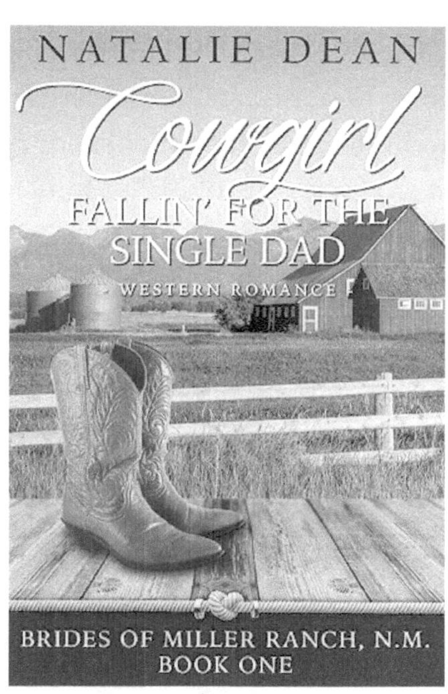

Hello readers! I hope you enjoyed the Miller Brothers of Texas series. This brings it to an end but I've still got one more Miller series for you! Cowgirl Brides of Miller Ranch, N.M. I love writing about the cowboys, but I thought it'd be fun to go out on a limb and write about cowgirls this time around.

Cowgirl Fallin' for the Single Dad brings you Charity Miller and the new doctor in town, Alejandro. He's tall, dark and handsome, and he also happens to be a single dad to sweet little girl named Savannah. This story is sure to warm your heart and rope you in to the new Miller series. It's got wonderful reviews and I think this might be one of my all time favorite Miller books. I hope you'll think so too!

You can find Charity and Alejandro's love story on all major retailers. But of course, as previously mentioned, it sure would be great if you could support my small bookstore. Scan the QR code below (might be on the next page, depending on the book format) to be taken to Cowgirl Fallin' for the Single Dad at Natalie Dean Books. If scanning QR codes isn't your thing, you can find my store here: nataliedeanbooks.com Just look under the Miller stories tab for Brides of Miller Ranch, N.M., and you should be able to find this book.

ABOUT THE AUTHOR

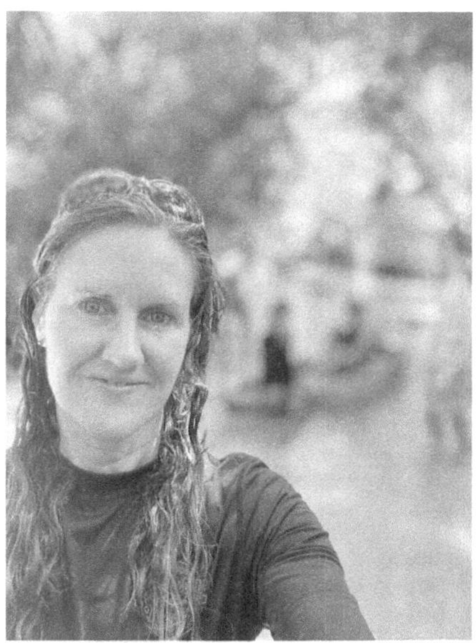

Born and raised in a small coastal town in the south, I was raised to treasure family and love the Lord. I'm a dedicated homeschooling mom who loves to travel and spend time with my growing-up-too-fast son.

When I'm not busy writing or running my business, you can find me cleaning house, cooking dinner, feeding our three rescue cats, trying to make learning fun and coaxing my son to pick up his toys. On less busy days, you may also find me paddling down a spring run in Florida, hiking a mountain trail in Georgia (on the rare vacation to the mountains), or enjoying a book.

If you love Natalie Dean books, you can be notified of new releases by signing up to my newsletter at nataliedeanau thor.com, where you will also receive two free short stories for signing up. Just click on the "Free Books" tab at the top and you'll be on your way!

Also, as previously mentioned, I've opened my own online bookstore and I'd love your support! As of June 2024, I'm selling my ebooks at Natalie Dean Books. By late summer or fall 2024, I should have audiobooks, regular paperbacks, large print paperbacks, dyslexic print paperbacks and signed paper-backs all available. At the request of my loyal readers, I'll also be adding merchandise, such as glasses, cups, magnets and more. So come check out my small mom-owned author busi-ness at nataliedeanbooks.com.

You can also scan the QR code below to be taken to the home page of Natalie Dean Books.

facebook.com/nataliedeanromance